10X 10/07 √2/09

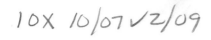

D0761947

APR 25 2002

My Suburban Shtetl

Library of Modern Jewish Literature

Other titles in the Library of Modern Jewish Literature

My Suburban
SHTETL

※

*A Novel about Life in a Twentieth-Century
Jewish-American Village*

ROBERT RAND

Syracuse University Press

First Edition 2001
02 03 04 05 06   6 5 4 3 2

The paper used in this publication meets the minimum requirements
of American National Standard for Information Sciences—
Permanence of Paper for Printed Library Materials, ANSI Z39.48–1984. ∞™

Library of Congress Cataloging-in-Publication Data
Rand, Robert.
My suburban shtetl : a novel about life in a twentieth-century
Jewish American village /
Robert Rand.—1st ed.
p. cm.
ISBN 0-8156-0721-0 (alk. paper)
1. Jews—United States—Fiction. 2. Suburban life—fiction. I. Title.
PS3618.A62 M9 2001
813'.54—dc21   2001042675

Manufactured in the United States of America

For Ariel

Robert Rand was senior editor of National Public Radio's *Weekend All Things Considered* from 1989 to 1997. He currently works as an independent public radio producer, journalist, and writer.

Contents

Acknowledgments

Thanks to the many friends and colleagues who were kind enough to read and comment on the manuscript of this novel as it was being created, or who endured my reading chapters of it aloud: Bob Fradkin, Goedele Gulikers, Mary Beth Kirchner, Sally Davies, Daniel Zwerdling, Fred Wasser, Bob Lyle, and the late Lynn Hamm. Thanks also to Sylvia and Terry Goggin, whose hospitality and recollections of childhood helped to spark the idea for this work.

My appreciation goes out to Robert Mandel and the folks at Syracuse University Press who embraced this project when others wouldn't. A special note of gratitude to Miriam Isaacs for Yiddish language assistance, and to Bruce Brigell of the Skokie Public Library. Thanks also to Arielle Eckstut, my literary agent, without whose encouragement this novel would never have been written. And to Annette Wenda, who made sure all the t's were crossed and the i's dotted.

My mom and dad, Florence and Al Rand, and my sister, Julie, contributed to this book in ways too numerous to count. To them I am most grateful. Thanks, too, to Van Schwab for assistance, and to the Holocaust survivors in Skokie who told me their stories. Finally, my biggest debt belongs to Eriko, my wife, who supported the writing of this novel without question, who endured the evolution of its chapters with patience and with well-placed editorial intervention, and whose love and affection formed the foundation of its creation. It is to Ariel—her son, and mine—that this book is dedicated.

My Suburban Shtetl

CHAPTER 1

Abe Yellin

G randpa's been arrested for hitting a Nazi with a salami!" The weapon, I later found out, was a Hebrew National all-beef projectile. One and a half feet long. Concrete-hard. Kosher, of course.

The sausage my grandpa, Abe Yellin, pulled out of his arsenal that day was thick and delicious with history:

In 1915, when Abe was young, the German army struck at his native Russia. At the time, Abe's world was no wider than the muddy street he crossed each morning to get to synagogue school. In class one day, as Abe was absorbed in his studies, a soldier marched in, a genuine Teuton dispatched by the kaiser to fortify the eastern front. The lad waved a bayonet, seized Abe by the arm, and told him to come along. Abe spent the rest of the First World War as a cook in a prisoner-of-war barracks.

Later, after the war, Abe emigrated to America and settled in Chicago. Honestly believing the fruit of his labor, even forced labor, was always sweet, Abe parlayed his wartime experience as a German mess hall chef into Yellin's Deli, the most revered Jewish eating establishment in Chicago's old West Side, 4059 West Roosevelt Road. Everybody knew the address by heart, and everybody's heart beat just a bit faster when they walked into the place, overcome as they were by the aroma of garlic and onion and hot-from-the-oven rye bread and everything good.

1

It was there, at the deli, that Abe developed a reputation for sausages. And when the second war against the Germans began, Abe cast aside his customary bent toward soft-spoken and reserved behavior and decided to act: he dispatched four dozen parcels of salamis overseas.

"Our boys are fighting the Nazis," he declared, "and empty stomachs are the last thing they need to worry about."

So it was that Yellin's salamis cheered many a GI and contributed to the defeat of Hitler.

And so it was natural now, in this summer of 1977, as the Nazis threatened to march again, that Abe Yellin—an *incensed* Abe Yellin—would reach into history and pull out the one weapon he knew to be particularly effective in beating back the Nazi threat: a Hebrew National hard-variety, kosher-caliber sausage.

I was, ironically, living in Germany when my sister telephoned with the news of Grandpa's arrest. I was there working for Radio Free Europe and Radio Liberty, whose headquarters were in Munich.

Munich had come a long way since the war. Once a center of Nazi life, the city had become a postwar showplace for modern German culture and democracy. It was home to a new generation of youth who wanted to challenge the past. "How could the Holocaust have happened?" they asked. "Were our parents responsible?"

Munich was also, to my mind and palate, a nice place to live. Lush Riesling wines and tart pilsner beer. *Apfelstrudel.* Oktoberfest. Blonde and brunette *mädchen* hip to the times and predisposed to sunbathe topless. A lovely posting, even for me, an American Jew.

Abe, of course, was troubled by my being there. He knew, as did I, that the click-click-clicks of goose-stepping Hitlerites still echoed in the ears of Munich's city elders. Every so often whiffs of prewar nostalgia reached the pages of local tabloids and spiked the discourse of beer-hall conversation. And the not-so-distant Sturm und Drang of the führer's public speeches still jostled my grandfather's sensibilities. Abe was just plain anxious about my well-being.

But he never voiced objections to my pursuits. On the contrary. The radios, he'd say, were doing God's work, broadcasting news to the subjugated, brainwashed, Communist-dominated, *anti-semitic* nations of the Soviet bloc. I was, in Abe's mind, a soldier, of sorts, on the freedom frontier: Bobby Bakalchuk, Jewish cold warrior, fighting the good fight against an evil nearly as loathsome as the Nazis. That's what he'd tell me. And that was the way he rationalized his grandson living on German soil.

There was, to my mind, no immediately apparent rationale for my grandpa's arrest. It was absurd, the notion that this former purveyor of deli meats, this gentle patriarch of foodstuffs and decency, might offend the law. My sister's call, on the face of it, made little sense. "What on earth are you talking about?" I asked her. "Grandpa arrested? Nazis? Salamis?"

Whereupon she proceeded to tell me what was befalling Skokie, Illinois, the village we grew up in, and the village Abe Yellin had called home for the past seventeen years.

It seems the controversy began when one Frank Collin, thirty-two, a narrow-minded but preternaturally determined man, concocted a plan to peddle his vision of America in Skokie. Collin, by outward appearance, hardly seemed a menace. He was a fresh-faced young fellow—fetching would not be entirely off the mark—with a swath of black hair and sad, moonstruck eyes that retreated, even cowered, in their sockets, suggesting a person who would rather be left alone. The man's appearance belied his calling, which was strident, aggressive, and patently unfriendly. Collin was a Nazi. A bona fide zieg heiler. He directed the National Socialist Party of America, which was based in Chicago, just south of Skokie. Collin's father, curiously, had survived the concentration camps, but had long ago disavowed the son.

Frank Collin had a straightforward view of the world: white Christians—he considered himself to be one—were superior beings; Jews and blacks were evil and had to be eliminated, or at least kept at bay. He wrapped his message in brownshirts, swastikas, and jackboots, and attracted an estimated one thousand followers around the country.

In Illinois, Collin's band of men consisted of two or three dozen storm troopers—that's what they called themselves. They were as crazy a bunch of misfits and society castoffs as there ever was. Dropouts. Jilted. Just plain angry white men. Their number was small. Many were still in their teens. But regardless of age, their propensity for hate was large. And they relished and flaunted the constitutionally protected right to spread their message anywhere the media might go, for it was media coverage that gave life to their theology and puffed up their egos.

In the spring of 1977, Collin asked Skokie for permission to stage a Nazi march on the streets of the village. He chose Skokie because a large number of Jews lived there, among them many thousands of Holocaust survivors. "Imagine the publicity!" Collin thought. The prospect gave him shivers and stirred him to the loins.

Skokie would have nothing of Frank Collin. The village dismissed his request by passing a hastily drafted series of ordinances: no parade permits to groups that dressed in military-style uniforms; no parade permits to groups that espoused hatred; no parade permits to any organization that failed to obtain $350,000 in liability insurance to cover losses or injury that might result from a public rally.

Collin rejected the village's tactics. He said he would march, come what may. The festivities, he said, would take place on Sunday, July Fourth.

Skokie, enraged, went to a judge, who issued an order enjoining the Independence Day demonstration.

"We respect the order of the court," Collin said. "There will be no July Fourth Nazi celebration."

Collin conspired to hold it instead on Saturday, July third. And on that day, at 10:00 A.M., Frank Collin and thirty of his cohorts packed themselves into four vehicles and headed north from Chicago on the Edens Expressway toward Skokie.

They met Abe Yellin and his salami at the Touhy Avenue exit.

Abe didn't stand alone that day. He was among a crowd of several hundred Skokie citizens, young and old, women and men, who had massed on the highway exit ramp at the edge of the village limits. At the core of the throng were the blessed ones, some of Skokie's most regarded, several score of aged Jews who had by their wits and by the charity of God survived the Holocaust. The survivors carried wood-pitched placards, their unsteady arms finding the strength to hoist the standards aloft. They shook the signs with agitation, up and down, over and over and over, like frenzied medieval infantrymen raising piked weapons for battle. The placards were white, and on them, in black hand-painted letters, these words: Dachau. Auschwitz. Berkinau. Bergen-Belsen. And as the survivors raised their banners, a shirt sleeve would slip down a wrist here and there, revealing different kinds of black, hand-painted marks—numbers—etched into their skin.

"Never again! Never again! Never again!" the survivors cried.

Police helicopters hung overhead as Collin, in the lead vehicle, drove toward the crowd. A plainclothes Skokie cop waved him down, and Collin got out of his car. He was dressed in a brown military uniform with a swastika armband coiled like a serpent around his left biceps.

"Sir, I'm advising you not to come here because we can't contain all these people," the officer said.

At which point the salami flew out of nowhere and speared Frank Collin point-first, dead center between the eyes.

"Look at me, you bastard," Abe said, having lurched through the crowd to position himself directly in front of the Nazi. Abe spoke so softly that only Collin and the arresting officer could hear, and his body trembled as he spoke, filled as it was with fury and with a sense that he had done something genuinely important.

"I'd like to crack your skull," Abe said. "That's the only way to deal with a snake like you. My sister and her entire family were murdered by you bastards."

When Abe was a boy, Mary had been his younger charge, not by necessity or by parental direction, but simply because Abe wanted it that way. She was his little sister, his only sister, his jewel, his joy, his mark, his muse, and he acted accordingly.

Mary was ten years younger than Abe. She was born in their mother's bed, and to this day, Abe—who had been in the next room when the baby first appeared—remembers his sister's first cries: loud, piercing howls like the wails of a shofar, the sacred ram's horn the rabbis sound to commemorate the Days of Awe. And it seemed to Abe that, like the shofar's wail, Mary's cries were both joyous and mournful, as if on the day of her birth she somehow knew that birth leads to death, and hers would be sudden, frightful, and premature.

Abe adored his little sister, who was by all accounts a beautiful child, with sensitive, delicate brown eyes, much like Abe's, and a smile, like Abe's, that was subtle but quick. Abe looked after her with uncommon gentleness. When Mary caught cold, Abe made her hot, black, sugared tea, which he administered by the spoonful as she lay in bed. When the August sun turned Mary's skin, which was porcelain white, into a palette of little brown freckles, Abe would rush out and buy salve from the old village healer, so Mary, who hated the splotches, could again play outside with self-assurance. And when the village bullies taunted Mary—for beautiful young girls always were taunted—calling her names or tossing stones in her direction, Abe would always intervene, covering his sister's ears so the names wouldn't register, taking the brunt of the assault himself, so the stones pelted him and not her.

Abe wasn't there to protect his sister in September 1942. He never forgave himself for that. The Nazi army had just marched into Lubeshov, the town of their birth. By then, Mary had taken a husband, a merchant named Julius, who ran a profitable flour mill there. It was because of the business that Mary and Julius never left the town.

"The Nazis herded all the Jewish families to the outskirts of the village, had them dig one long grave, stripped all adults and children naked, and shot them dead with machine guns," Abe later told me. "Mary's three children, aged ten, eight, and six, her husband's parents, and possibly two hundred other Jewish families perished in one day. One of my cousins somehow crawled out of the mass grave alive and escaped into the forest. He later made his way to Israel, where he wrote me of the horror he had lived through."

Abe had a photograph of Mary: a black-and-white print taken when she was sixteen. The Red Cross delivered the picture to him, along with a letter, in 1941.

"I want you to have this," Mary wrote. "And don't worry about us. We're going to be all right."

The photo, now tattered, was always with Abe, tucked inside his wallet. He reached for it, without thinking, and studied his sister's face as he rode in the police car to the Skokie lockup to be booked for the assault on Frank Collin.

My sister said that Grandpa's arrest had made big news back

home. "Lead story in the *Chicago Tribune*," she said. "It was even on the national network nightly news. Grandpa looked so strange, handcuffed and all."

The simple assault and battery—that's what Abe was charged with—had stopped Frank Collin cold turkey. The leader of the National Socialist Party of America spit at my grandfather's feet, removed a bit of sausage fat from the bridge of his nose, got back into his car, and headed home to Chicago to regroup for another fight another day.

Abe pleaded guilty to the charges against him. He was fined twenty-five dollars, and promptly released. The judge characterized Abe's action as "factually outside the law, but understandable under the circumstances." Abe left the courthouse bolstered by the cheers of the throng that had gathered there, still a bit shaken by the uncharacteristic temerity he had exhibited that day, and resolute in his conviction that Frank Collin would never, ever march in Skokie.

My grandfather was not the kind of fellow you'd figure to thrust himself into a political whirlwind. He valued modesty, restraint, and, above all, reason. He was about as rambunctious as a teddy bear.

As kids, me and my sister used to think of Abe as our very own Winnie-the-Pooh. He looked like the A. A. Milne character, a bit short and stout, roly-poly in an Old Country kind of way. A face, like Pooh's, that emanated warmth and love and a palpable sense of calm. A voice that drew you in with its modesty and humor. He even felt furry when we held him.

But a man of action? A take-to-the-streets vigilante? A practitioner of violence, even though the cause is worthy? That wasn't the Abe I spent so much of my childhood with.

My grandfather was a poet—a philosopher, really. He once described himself as "a good listener, but a slow talker; a prolific writer, but a poor conversationalist." A few simple words or a silly rhyme. That was the way he made sense of the world:

Oh, birdie! Be honest and fair,
Tell me, what keeps you up in the air?
I would trade you many, many things,
For your skill and flapping wings;

When you're hungry, you get your food free,
In bad weather, you find shelter in a tree;
You always sing—never cry,
When you see danger, you take off to the sky;

You build your nest with your little mouth,
Comes winter, you fly south;
Tell me, birdie, what can I do,
To be content, happy and free like you?

Abe delighted in aphorisms. He'd write them down long-hand on little three-by-five note cards and have them delivered special by mail.

"Wisdom is a rare commodity, but you can get it free if you strive for it," he'd write. "If you want to be smart, you have to make a start. If you want to advance, you have to use common sense. If you want something to grow, you must irrigate and sow."

"Mr. Postman," he'd say, handing over a card, aphorism on one side, neatly penned address and stamp on the other, "my grandson seems troubled these days. This will help. Please see that it's promptly delivered."

"Yes, Mr. Yellin. Will do."

Thus did my grandpa dispatch considerable wisdom and ensure the emotional grounding of his clan.

If there was anyone in the family likely to stir controversy, it was Abe's wife, Emma, my grandmother. She was an organizer and doer, constantly working the neighborhood, arranging teas, hosting literary salons, attending Jewish functions, inviting friends and acquaintances over for lunch, often without reciprocation.

Emma was also an opinionated woman with a tongue that could wag with the best of them. "Oh, that Weinstein. How can you stand him, Abe? He goes to the movies on the Sabbath!" Or: "That Lieberman woman. You treat her so kindly, Abe, yet she's nothing but an old hen with no purpose in life other than to eat my sponge cake without once even telling me how tasty it is." Or: "Mr. Horowitz, *your good friend* Mr. Horowitz, didn't acknowledge your birthday, Abe. He's a piece of *drek,* and I told him so."

Abe loved Emma dearly, though she did speak her mind. And worse still, she loved to dance. This latter affliction caused Abe much consternation. Especially at family gatherings.

"Come, Abe," Emma would say, dropping the latest Benny Goodman vinyl onto the turntable. "Let's cut up the rug."

She'd hold out her arms and beckon her mate until Abe would nearly burst with embarrassment, surrounded as he was by his daughters and grandchildren and brothers and in-laws of various stripes and degrees, all of whom knew that Abe was a private man who just hated to dance. And Emma would persist until Abe relented, and he'd stand there, on the makeshift living-room dance floor, his legs rigid, his body swaying ever so slightly as he tripped over the left-pause, right-pause, rock-back rhythm of a six-count swing; and his arms would flap up and down as Emma led him through turns and twists, and his face would flush with humiliation. And we'd all applaud when the ordeal was over, and Emma would hug Abe, and Abe would smile and forgive his wife for ruffling his pride and sense of tranquillity.

It was Emma who answered the phone when I called from Munich to speak with my grandpa to learn more about his arrest.

"How's he doing, Grandma?" I asked.

"Nazis. In Skokie. How do you think he's doing? Abe, come here. Bobby's on the phone from Germany."

Abe took the phone. I heard him sigh.

"Grandpa, are you okay?"

"Yes, yes, I'm fine. No need to worry. How are you?"

"Listen, were you hurt or anything?"

"No, no. I'm fine."

"How did it happen?"

He paused, acknowledging with silence that this was a serious question that deserved a thoughtful answer. Another sigh, then:

"It had to happen," he said. "Skokie is our home. We have a good life here, a quiet life. We can be Jews here. Our shul is here. This place is a sanctuary for our friends who survived the camps. They are happy here, and we are honored to have them among us. No German, no Nazi, is going to tarnish that or take that away. Never."

Grandpa spoke gently and with composure. But there was a cold, sharp, unyielding edge to his voice, something I'd never heard before. It was as if his conscience, stooped but comfortable after seventy-plus years of life, had suddenly twisted upright, and the stiffening had caused pain.

"Experience teaches," he continued. "Columbus discovered that the earth is round in shape. What he didn't discover is that the system that drives the earth is also circular. Day follows night, and night follows day. Year follows year. Life follows death by birth, starting the life cycle over again. In the world order, peace follows war—but after a period of peace, war breaks out again. The Almighty, in his wisdom, gives us the opportunity to learn through repetition, to read the lessons of history over and over again, to digest them and to apply the knowledge we gain for the betterment of mankind. It is our greatest test to recognize this and to act accordingly. But sometimes we fail to read these cycles properly. We fail to remember that experience teaches. So right now, here in our own village, a cycle begins again, and again we are called on to reflect, to learn, to respond. A man and his storm troopers want to wave swastikas in our collective face. This snake, this Collin, wants to defile us, to spit on the memory of the six million who died, to assault and shatter the peace of mind of those here who survived the Holocaust. I stood helpless in the war as my sister was murdered. I stood helpless before that in my own little town, in my shtetl, my Lubeshov, as a German even younger than you walked into school and dragged me away with all the compassion of a thief snatching a loaf of bread. Experience teaches. The Nazis will not march here. I did not move to Skokie for that."

As I sat there in Munich, considering Abe's words, I realized that my grandfather had found, in the village of my own childhood, a connection, and a powerful one at that, to the place in which he was reared. Skokie was his Lubeshov, or the Lubeshov, rather, that should have been. In Skokie, Abe had found the peace and calm and sustenance and security that had been taken from him as a youth, and from his family who remained in Russia after that. In Skokie, Abe lived in happy retirement, a thinker and poet no longer encumbered by the burdens of running a business or of feeding a young family. He spent his time studying and wondering and reading and writing and living a Jewish life, much as he had done as a young teenager before the first war. He was the happiest he'd ever been, and I, as the grandchild who grew up by him, had benefited from that good spirit, and all the kindness and wisdom that came with it.

Abe had a bond to Skokie, and through it, a line to his own

past. The Nazi controversy had forced him to look back on the cycles he'd seen in his life and to declare, publicly and irrevocably, that some things just could not stand. It was a defining moment for my grandfather, and I was proud of him for it. And I found myself wondering, after I'd said good-bye to Abe, how Skokie, and the people and events I'd experienced there with him, had shaped my own sense of what is right and what is wrong, of what or who can be tolerated, and of what or who cannot. And I recalled my youth, and looked back in my mind for some answers.

CHAPTER 2

Norman-Meyer

N orman-Meyer Ashkenaz was a cootie. That's what we kids called him back in 1962, when JFK was president, when Skokie was writing the American dream, when we were ten years old. We didn't really know for sure why we used the word, or what the dictionary meaning of it was. (Webster, by the way, defines *cootie* as "a body louse.") We just knew that cooties were part of the general kid population and were pretty much to be avoided. Or at least ridiculed in a merciless kid kind of way.

Norman-Meyer was a cootie mainly because of his looks. His hair was red and curly, and he stood out because of that. And he was fat. Double-chin fat. Belly-flesh-bulging-through-your-clothes kind of fat. Smell-a-lot-when-you-get-sweaty-in-gym-class fat. Because of his weight, Norman-Meyer waddled around the halls of our school, East Prairie Grammar and Junior High, in constant sartorial disarray. His shirts would fight the confinement of his belts, coming partially untucked and unbuttoned by morning recess. His pants, which struggled to contain the girth of his gut, seemed to screech and groan as they battled to hold Norman-Meyer together. And his socks would slump toward his feet, their elastic grip loosened by the bulk of his ankles. He was, in short, a human rumple, and a rather substantial one at that.

Besides his looks, Norman-Meyer's name was unusual to our

ears, and that also contributed to his precarious social status. Why on earth, we wondered, did he need two first names? It was clearly a case of cooties.

The reason behind all this lay with Norman-Meyer's parents, of course. They were a tempestuous, poorly matched couple, and they rarely agreed about anything. When their one and only child was born, they couldn't decide what to call him. It was a given, of course, that their son would be named after an honored, deceased relative. Such was the Jewish tradition, and there was no bickering over that. But which relative? Should it be the recently departed paternal great-uncle, Norman Ashkenaz? Or Meyer Rabinowitz, the esteemed maternal great-great-grandfather?

Oh, how Norman-Meyer's parents fought over this decision! His father, Joseph, from whom Norman-Meyer got his red hair, screamed and yelled and cursed and threatened. "My son will carry my family's name, you bitch!" he shouted at his wife. Norman-Meyer's mother, Fanya, sat there silently, as she usually did, in stoic defiance. She wouldn't give in. So three weeks after Norman-Meyer was born, a rabbi was found to resolve the controversy over "the baby Ashkenaz." The rabbi's name was Vevel-Zalman Ginzburg. Thus was Joseph and Fanya's offspring dubbed Norman-Meyer.

Rabbi Ginzburg, in all his wisdom, was no Soloman, for he overlooked the unfortunate titular similarity between Norman-Meyer and *Oscar* Meyer, ostensible chief executive officer of the most famous hot dog and luncheon meat manufacturer in the world. The oversight was the source of much glee for us kids and a certain degree of misery for Norman-Meyer.

"Oscar Meyer, Oscar Meyer, how's your wiener?" we'd shout whenever Norman-Meyer walked by. And as if by divine intervention, Norman-Meyer forgot to zip up one day, and his Norman-Meyerhood, such as it was, poked out of a pair of red-and-white-striped boxer shorts for all of us to see.

"I wish I had a Norman-Meyer wiener," we later sang. *"Tiny and all purple it would be-ee-ee. And if I had a Norman-Meyer wiener, I would never ever have to pee!"*

On top of all this, Norman-Meyer was visually impaired. In order to see he wore heavy, tortoise-shell glasses with dense, parabolic lenses that looked like the bottoms of soda pop bottles. He was quite a sight to behold. I once told him, stupidly, that he had "cootie eyes" because of the way the lenses distorted his pupils: from the outside looking in, his eyes appeared to be two times their normal size. You never knew how Norman-Meyer took to such comments, though. His gaze appeared blurred by those glasses of his, his feelings masked by a bifocal curtain.

My relationship with Norman-Meyer Ashkenaz was complicated by the fact that I liked him. We were neighbors, and had been ever since 1954, when our parents first moved to Skokie. As babies we'd stare and drool at each other from adjacent strollers as our mothers walked the neighborhood, or we'd examine each other's feet when Fanya came over for tea and Norman-Meyer shared my playpen. Later, once we'd grown into little kids, we'd play together all day long as little kids do, digging up the ground looking for worms, chasing imaginary ghouls and goblins, lying on the grass, staring straight up into the sky and finding faces in the clouds. Norman-Meyer's vision had already turned bad by then, and he had, I believed, trouble discerning those clouds. So I felt obliged to describe to him with impeccable meteorological accuracy exactly what was there. "Norman-Meyer," I'd say, "see that big old white cloud there? It's what they call a *serious* cloud, and it's made up of ice crystals and things, and if you look at it sideways it kind of looks like my Grandpa Abe, doncha think?"

And Norman-Meyer would nod and smile, because he liked my Grandpa Abe, who treated him kindly and gave him presents. And he also knew, even with his vision, that the cirrus cloud was really a cumulus cloud, but he was too polite to tell me.

Norman-Meyer was like that. He had knowledge and understanding beyond his years. But he never used those gifts to embarrass me, even when I embarrassed him, like the times I'd join the kids at school in administering pretend cootie shots to inoculate ourselves against catching Norman-Meyer's terrible condition.

Norman-Meyer understood me better than I understood myself. He knew that I was terribly shy and insecure and needed to be popular by going along. So he didn't deprive me, and he'd suffer the consequent taunting in silence. And though he'd sometimes chide me when we were alone together— "Bobby, is your cootie shot still good? Because I wouldn't want you to catch cooties from me today!"—he never made an issue of it in public, for he didn't want to make me feel uncomfortable. He'd seen his father humiliate his mother enough times to know that emotional discomfort can hurt, and he was too sensitive a soul to upset anyone. Besides, I was his only friend. So Norman-Meyer and I coexisted in the complicated kind of way that human beings do.

We lived, back then, on Jarvis Street, on the southern edge of a village that was feeding off the postwar prosperity that much of white America enjoyed. In the early fifties, GIs could get cheap loans to purchase affordable housing in the suburbs, and they swarmed to Skokie from Chicago, young wives in tow, to build their castles, tend their lawns, and realize their dreams.

My father, who'd served with Patton during World War II, once told me that he moved to Skokie to buy a house with a staircase. That was his dream. "Most Jewish people were raised in apartments," he said. "And I was, too. But I always wanted something more, something like the movies. *Gone with the Wind,* you know? A home with style, with an upstairs and a downstairs and an elegant, flowing, spiraling staircase in between."

Norman-Meyer's parents moved to Skokie for reasons less idyllic: they were evicted from their Chicago apartment because Joseph, Norman-Meyer's father, repeatedly punched holes in the flat's drywall with his fist. Their landlord, Mr. Seligman, made light of the first hole, which was reported by Mrs. Scharfman, the building know-it-all. "We're all entitled to get a little angry once in a while," Mr. Seligman said. But then old Mrs. Siegel, who lived alone in the apartment next to the Ashkenaz family, was awakened one night by terrible shouting next door, and as she sat up in bed to listen to the commotion, split-splat came Joseph Ashkenaz's knuckles right into her boudoir. "Get out, Ashkenaz!" Mr. Seligman said the next day, after hearing from Mrs. Siegel. So Joseph, having little recourse, collected his family and headed north to Skokie, where Jews were beginning to settle, where nobody knew him, and where the effects of his anger could be confined to his new single-family home.

New residents, like my parents and Norman-Meyer's, moved into Skokie in droves in the fifties, at the rate, a village newspaper reported, of nearly one an hour. At the beginning of the decade, 12,500 people lived there. By 1962, the population had soared to 65,000. The demand for housing was so great that developers built ten or twelve units on plots of land designed to hold eight. The extra houses were stuffed in sideways, their front doors facing the bricks of neighboring buildings instead of the street.

The homes were plain and defined middle class. Some had second-floor staircases, like ours. But most, like Norman-Meyer's, were one-story buildings with beige bricks, brown or gray shingled pitched roofs, and rectangular picture windows

that gazed out over little green patches of front yard. Occasionally, architects cut weird-looking, obtuse, triangular glass por-
tals into the front doors of these houses. It was a touch of
glamour, they said, as if Kandinsky or Picasso had visited there.

An economic rush accompanied the housing boom in
Skokie, and by the end of the fifties the village had become "one
of the gasket capitals of the world," thanks to a company called
Fel-Pro, which placed a plant there. "It's a fact: every modern car
today is equipped with one or more gaskets from Fel-Pro," their
advertisement read. So it was that Skokie rivaled only Detroit in
putting America on wheels. And so it was that Congregation
Bnai Emunah, one of the first synagogues to open in Skokie, established the Fel-Pro Brotherhood, a social organization of tem-
ple-goers who all happened to work at Fel-Pro. The
brotherhood was famous for its bowling team and for sponsor-
ship of the annual "Bagel Hop Dance."

Among the other big-name businesses that called Skokie
home were Rand McNally, Allstate Insurance, G. D. Searle, and
the Teletype Corporation. We were thankful that village plan-
ners zoned these and other companies in out-of-the-way places,
so we didn't even know they were there. Their tax dollars, however, did ensure that Norman-Meyer and I attended top-quality
schools that could afford the best teachers and the latest in
overhead-projector technology.

Before the postwar explosions in housing and business,
Skokie resembled a worked-over swamp. Literally. The
Potawatomi Indians originally settled the land in the eighteenth
century, and the terrain they lived on was soft and mushy, satu-
rated by the underground reach of Lake Michigan to the east.
The name *Skokie*, in fact, derives from the Potawatomi word for
"big swamp." The Indians made a go of it for a while, hunting
game and the like. I remember the day Norman-Meyer and I
were helping my mother till her garden when she hit a stone

with her hoe—except that upon close examination it wasn't a stone, but a genuine arrowhead surely of Potawatomi origin. My mother gave it to me and I gave it to Norman-Meyer, for he'd never seen an arrowhead before, whereas I had, during a trip to the natural history museum with my grandpa Abe. And after this archaeological discovery, Norman-Meyer and I attached the arrowhead to a stick and pretended we were Potawatomi braves. We'd stalk around the neighborhood oh so quietly in our bare feet, so as not to startle the make-believe bear we were tracking. We did startle a scantily clad Mrs. Epstein once, who was sunning herself in her backyard and didn't appreciate the intrusion.

"Sorry, Mrs. Epstein," I said. "We're just hunting for bear."

"Get out of here, boys," she said, "or I'll tell Norman-Meyer's father you're up to no good."

And we quickly retreated, much as the Potawatomi did in the nineteenth century when the first white settlers came to Skokie. The settlers were primarily Germans and Prussians, men called Heinrich Harms and Peter Blameuser. They built cabins and drained the swamplands and put up farms and churches and general stores and greenhouses. The area prospered. And soon Skokie became one of the largest truck-farming regions in the country, shipping pigs and poultry and fruits and vegetables south to Chicago over a rickety system of wooden plank roads that eventually gave way to the railroad and to paved thoroughfares. By the late 1920s, the village had five thousand residents, six public schools, a new village hall, and sixty-one speakeasies.

It also had movies, for before there was Hollywood, there was Skokie. I learned this by happenstance one Sunday afternoon, when Norman-Meyer and I took the bus over to the Skokie Theater for a kids' matinee. We liked that old movie house. It was tiny—"capacity 100"—and had luxury push-back seats. We'd sit in the front row, so Norman-Meyer could see better, and stare up at that big, old quasi-technorama screen with root beers in one hand and popcorn in the other, and there just wasn't a better time to be had by a kid on a Sunday afternoon. On that particular day, the theater was featuring films of the silent era, and topping the bill was a western called *The Clutching Hand*, starring the great turn-of-the-century actress Pauline Frederick. I don't remember much about the plot, but I do remember this fact: the movie was filmed in Skokie. It even said so, right there at the end of the film, in the credits.

Turns out that back in the teens, at the very time Abe Yellin was a young student in Lubeshov, Skokie was a young industry's proving ground. The village resembled an old western town, with dusty dirt roads and saloons, and George K. Spoor and Broncho Billy Anderson, owners of the Chicago-based Essanay Film Manufacturing Company, decided to shoot westerns there. They dispatched wagon loads of silent-film stars and camera crews to the town center, and what a terrific set it made. There, at the intersection of Lincoln Avenue and Oakton Street, right by the old village bank building and down the block from where the Skokie Theater would later stand, they'd film shootouts between cowboys and Indians or sheriffs and bank robbers. A. J. Lindermann, a village vegetable grower, later recalled: "We kids got so used to seeing ambushes and men tied to trees with arrows going right through them that we considered it a very normal part of the scenery."

But Skokie was to be no more than an asterisk in the history of America's film industry. George and Broncho Billy would move their whole operation to Hollywood, where they signed Charlie Chaplin. And by 1920, the streets of my town had been emptied of sagebrush, and village life returned to normal again.

Skokie raced through the twenties with the wind of big-time prosperity at its back. It was a good era, characterized by much growth. A chamber of commerce was founded. Local newspapers began publishing. A women's club was organized. But the village crashed in 1929 along with the rest of the country, and in the thirties it just plain stopped growing altogether. The cement streets and sidewalks that optimistic developers had put in to support anticipated housing simply lay there, giant crisscross grids cutting through wide-open prairies. The land would remain fallow until after the Second World War, when good fortune returned, and Skokie began to recover.

Abe Yellin moved into Skokie in 1960, after selling his Roosevelt Road delicatessen. He and my grandma Emma bought a modest retirement home a few blocks away from us, within walking distance of Temple Shalom, the local synagogue.

Abe was immediately comfortable in Skokie. Not only did his grandson live nearby, but Jews inhabited virtually every single dwelling spot in the neighborhood. There were the Cohens and the Liechtensteins and the Zimmers and the Marguleses. The Schwabs and the Brownsteins were there, along with the Levy and Milstein families. Rabbi Green, my Hebrew-school teacher, honored our street by purchasing a home there in 1958. And Morton Silver, the village *mohel,* was there, and what a busy *mohel* he was back in those baby-boom days, circumcising eight-day-old Jewish males with the speed and precision of a surgeon and the glee of a prospector who'd finally struck gold.

There was no Moses who led the Jews to Skokie. But to the Jewish families who settled there, it was a land of milk and honey. They came from the Jewish ghettos of Chicago's South and West Sides, a handful first in the early postwar years. In 1952, when the first organized Jewish religious service was held in Skokie, barely a hundred Jewish families lived there. But by the sixties, a demographic revolution was under way, with half a dozen synagogues supporting a Jewish population that was in the tens of thousands. Among them were many hundreds of

Holocaust survivors. By the time Frank Collin planned his Nazi march, the number of survivor families had swelled to as many as seven thousand, and an estimated 40 to 50 percent of all village residents were Jewish, an extraordinarily high number for any American community.

They came to Skokie because other Jews came before them. They came because life there was good, with safe streets where kids could play ball, with backyards that had willow trees and patios and a whiff of barbecue in the air, with synagogues where their kids, like me and Norman-Meyer, could study Hebrew and learn Torah and become bar mitzvahed. And they came because Chicago began to look different, because the great migration of African Americans from the South that had started years earlier had finally begun to alter the racial texture of their old neighborhoods. "The West Side was changing," they'd say. And everybody understood. The old Jewish ghettos were turning into something else.

My mother, Abe's daughter Miriam, took to Skokie with all the grace and ease that the fifties demanded of her. She cooked and baked and cleaned and joined the PTA and the temple sisterhood. She taught me and my sister and even Norman-Meyer how to play the piano. And when time would allow, she'd paint—wonderful, bright watercolors of fruit or flowers, or oil portraits of her friends. And Miriam was stunning. Drop-dead beautiful, with jet-black, wavy hair, a Grace Kelly figure, and brown eyes that had the power to reduce my father to jelly. All in all, she was quite a package. So nobody was surprised when in March 1959 a local newspaper, the *Skokie News*, named Miriam Bakalchuk "Pin Up Mother" of the week:

> Mrs. Jacob Bakalchuk, 305 Jarvis, is just completing her first year as treasurer of the East Prairie PTA. Tall, dignified and refined in her manner, attractive Miriam also directs the Tem-

ple Shalom sisterhood organization. There she has organized bake sales and art auctions, and has even on occasion performed piano recitals, the proceeds of which have been used to plant trees in Israel.

Mrs. Bakalchuk graduated from the Chicago Academy of Fine Arts, with honors, and worked as a waitress at Yellin's Deli, her parents' restaurant in Chicago. There she met Jacob, her husband. They have been married for nine years and are very happy. Jacob is in sales.

Miriam keeps a joyful, neat home, gets the family off to work or school in the morning with a pat on the back if needed, after preparing a hearty breakfast.

She is friendly, gracious, courteous and kind, and grateful to those with whom she has worked in various enterprises.

Beneath the article was a photograph of Miriam "with her two good-looking children, Robert and Deborah."

Fanya, Norman-Meyer's mother, posted the article on the door of her refrigerator, for she was proud of Miriam, whom she considered her confidante and best friend. Miriam, in fact, was Fanya's lifeline, the one person, besides Norman-Meyer, who allowed her to breathe. My mom included Fanya in as many activities as Fanya believed she could handle without upsetting Joseph, her husband. The two women, for instance, both loved to cook, and on the eve of Jewish holidays they'd spend hours together in our kitchen, preparing huge vats of chicken soup and *tsimmes* and gefilte fish and kasha.

"Enjoy, enjoy, Miriam," Fanya would say, refusing to take all but a small packet of food home. "Give Abe and Emma my very best. Tell Abe I stewed the carrots special for him. I know how he loves them with his fish." And later, while we were all feasting at my grandparents' house, reciting the prayers and singing the songs of Rosh Hashanah or Hanukkah or Passover, Fanya would sit at her own kitchen table, silently, as Joseph devoured his meal quickly and without comment, and as Norman-Meyer sat there blank-faced, asking for seconds and thirds.

Fanya's favorite activity with Miriam was mah-jongg. The game was of Chinese origin, but to judge from the zeal with which Skokie women played it, you'd think that the Israelites had received it from atop Mount Sinai.

The game, from my ten-year-old perspective, was a complicated affair. Four women—Miriam; Fanya; Rabbi Green's wife, Anita; and Irma, the butcher's wife—would gather together one night a week, usually Mondays, in the living room of our home, and huddle around a fold-up card table, with twelve dozen domino-like marble tiles before them. The tiles were wonderful things, their faces etched with brightly colored pictures, beautiful Oriental images of dragons and flowers and even the wind.

The tiles made the most pleasing sound when the ladies mixed them together in the center of the table, a wondrous clatter like monotonal wind chimes. I often fell asleep to the music of those tiles, which I could hear from my bedroom nearby.

I also remember the strange, exotic words the women uttered once the match was under way. "I'll take the three bam." "Four crack." "Red dragon." "Mahj!" To this day I don't know what the object of their game was, or what mysterious tricks they played to win. But I do know that every one of them, especially Fanya, really enjoyed herself.

Although Norman-Meyer and I spent lots of time together, I never really got to know his mom. I could tell she was different from the other moms, though. Her son was different, for one. And she was older than the other moms, and grayer, too. And she hardly ever laughed, despite my best efforts.

"Mrs. Ashkenaz, Mrs. Ashkenaz," I'd say.

"Yes, Bobby dear, what is it?"

"Knock knock."

"Who's there?"

"Ahch."

"Ahch who?"

"God bless you!"

Whereupon I would proceed to giggle at the power of my wit, and Norman-Meyer would squeal like a pork belly that had been poked in the ribs. But all Fanya could manage was a Mona Lisa smile and a little shrug of the shoulder. "Come, kids," she'd say. "Have some ice cream. I have vanilla, I have chocolate, I have strawberry. Only I don't have luck."

My Grandpa Abe once told me that I should always be extra kind to Fanya, even if she didn't laugh at my jokes. "For some people life is more difficult than for others," he said. "A man is rich who is happy with his lot, but one may be lucky, another may not. Fanya is among the unlucky, Bobby."

"Why is she unlucky, Grandpa?" I asked.

He paused, as was his habit before answering questions, then said, "Sit down."

I took a place on his living room couch.

"What do you hear?" he asked me.

I listened for a moment. "I don't hear anything, Grandpa."

"Listen again," he said, "this time closely."

I screwed up my nose in determination, for this was a challenge, then mustered all the attention I had in my ears. And I listened. But again, I heard nothing.

"Sorry, Grandpa, I still don't hear anything."

"You hear silence, Bobby. You hear the sound of peace that fills our household, and that fills yours as well. Always remember that sound, for it is the source of happiness, and we are blessed to have it. It is the sound our rabbis called *shalom bayis*, the peaceful home, and it springs from love and respect and harmony and goodwill, and it thrives when a husband loves his wife as much as himself, and honors her as well; but it withers when anger, suspicion, and resentment seep into the home and shatter the silence. Do you understand what I'm saying?"

"Well, sort of," I said. "You mean that Norman-Meyer doesn't have a quiet home?"

"I suspect that is the case," Abe said. "And I suspect, too, that one of the reasons Norman-Meyer likes you so much, and one of the reasons he and his mother visit your house so often, is that the peace that speaks there speaks to them, too, and they like the sound, even though they, like you, cannot hear it."

And I left my grandpa's home that day intent on listening more closely to the things and people around me, for I'd realized that even in silence there are worlds to be discovered. And I headed out in search of Norman-Meyer, determined to bring him to the most silent, peaceful, wonderful, scary place in Skokie I knew: the Emily Park lagoon.

The lagoon was unlike anything else in Skokie. Frogs lived there. So did turtles and snakes and dragonflies and even the occasional owl. Fish swam in the lagoon's waters. And the cattails that grew at the water's edge were so thick and tall and inviting that a kid just couldn't help but enter their embrace, at considerable risk of getting lost forever. During the summertime you could pay a dollar and take a rowboat out on the lagoon and just sit there and enjoy the quiet warmth of the sun and the cadence of the cicadas, whose high-pitched song would drone out the occasional *blurp-blurp* of a pond toad. In the winter, the lagoon would freeze over and you could ice skate from one end to the other and hear nothing but the swoosh of your blades as they cut into the gray hush of the cold afternoon.

I especially liked the lagoon at night, for at night, when it was most quiet, you could close your eyes and see the history of the place. And you could imagine what it was like there in 1934, when Baby Face Nelson was murdered, and his gold-plated sidearm was dumped into the lagoon's silty waters.

The body of George "Baby Face" Nelson—born Lester Gillis—was actually found about a half-mile northwest of the lagoon, on the northern edge of St. Paul's Cemetery. There is no disputing how the gangster died.

It happened on November 27. At the time, Nelson was the most widely sought criminal in the United States. The government officially called him Public Enemy Number One. Nobody, not Pretty Boy Floyd or Clyde Barrow or Bonnie Parker, all of whom were on the loose back then, was wanted more. Law enforcement officials said that Baby Face was a merciless killer, a quick triggerman who passionately despised "coppers and G-men." He killed with submachine guns. But he slept with that gold-plated pistol under his pillow, and carried the weapon on him at all times.

On the day in question, two federal agents, Herman E. Hollis and Samuel P. Cowley, had cornered Nelson and several companions near a town called Barrington, located several miles north of Skokie. There was a shootout. A really bad one. Hollis and Cowley were killed, but not before hitting their prey. Baby Face took seventeen bullets. His companions, including his wife, Helen, stuffed Nelson's near-lifeless body into the agents' car and fled south.

The next morning, a Chicago undertaker named Philip Sadowski received a telephone call.

"Hello, is this you, Phil?" the caller said.

"Yes," Sadowski replied.

"Phil, I want you to go out to Harms Road near Lincoln Avenue in Skokie. You'll find a body there on the parkway. It's a friend of mine. His name is Gillis, and he's been hurt bad."

Sadowski notified Ambrose Brod, the Skokie police commissioner, who along with federal agents went looking for the body. They found it at the corner of Long and Niles Avenues, on the northern edge of the cemetery, near the graves of Helmuth Hollinger and the Windelborn family. The body was naked, a blanket its only shield against the elements, except for a strip of white cloth that was wrapped around Nelson's belly, where there was a gaping wound.

"His body was stained with blood," the *New York Times* reported the next day. "Nelson's arms were twisted and his generally cheerful face was contorted. It was apparent that he died in intense agony.

"An examination disclosed that the skin of the tips of three fingers had been filed, as if to change their texture, and the little finger of the right hand appeared to have been treated with acid, probably for the same purpose."

Nelson's clothing was found later that afternoon, dumped in a package on Howard Street, near the Emily Park lagoon. "A zipper belt on the trousers, probably used as a money container, had been cut open and its contents removed," the *Times* reported. The holster that carried the gold-plated sidearm was also empty.

J. Edgar Hoover, chief of the Justice Department's Division of Investigation, officially confirmed Nelson's death. "Yes, we got the guy," Hoover said. "But he killed two of our men. It was two lives for one."

The government automobile that Nelson's companions had used to transport Baby Face was eventually found near Winnetka, another Chicago suburb. Most of the missing money showed up in Nelson's wife's boudoir. But Nelson's prized possession, the gold-plated pistol, was never recovered. The proximity of the lagoon to St. Paul's Cemetery, and especially to the place where Nelson's clothes were dumped, led several generations of Skokie boys to one indisputably obvious conclusion: the pistol lay in the mud and muck of the lagoon's bottom, just for the taking.

And I was convinced that Norman-Meyer would help me take it. If only I could get him to the lagoon.

The lagoon, you see, had developed a bad reputation in the years following Baby Face Nelson's demise. Nasty people were rumored to hang out there, sexual perverts of various sorts who played with themselves and preyed on unsuspecting little kids walking to school. What's more, an occasional car was found lilting in the lagoon waters, the result of who knew what kind of evil. And then there was the case of seven-year-old Billy Cohen, who, in the spring of 1957, was playing at the lagoon with a third grader named Irwin Miller, who was mentally retarded. Irwin pushed Billy into the water, which sucked Billy downward with a mysterious force that nobody could really explain. The police had to pull Billy's body out of the lagoon with ropes, so ensnared was it in the mud.

Afterward, Mordechai Rappoport, the Orthodox rabbi, pronounced the lagoon off-limits to all Jews. "It is an evil place and ye shall not go there. *Tui, tui, tui!*" he declared.

Reb Rappoport, as he was called, was the local prophet and collector of monies for Judaism. He was an old man with an old-style wide-brimmed hat and a long, gray beard, one of those beards that was unkempt and fuzzy and reached down to the belt buckle. He dressed in black clothing and walked the streets all day long with a cane in one hand and a cup in the other, knocking on Jewish doors in search of funds for this or that cause. And he always had something sagacious to tell you, whether you wanted to hear it or not.

"Mrs. Ashkenaz," he'd say, "you should pray a bit harder, for blessed be he who serves the Lord our God with all his heart. *Tui, tui, tui!*" Or: "Mrs. Yellin, love the Lord your God with all your heart, but you will have a cold winter if you don't contribute more than a quarter. *Tui, tui, tui!*" Or: "Mrs. Bakalchuk, remember all the commandments of the Lord and do them, and you should wear your skirts a bit longer, too. *Tui, tui, tui!*"

Nobody ever took Reb Rappoport seriously. Until Billy Cohen died. Then his words, at least his words about the lagoon, seemed, to our parents, to make sense. Miriam, my mom, told me to stay away from Emily Park. But I ignored her appeal. The place was just too wonderful, and too close to our house, to abandon. But Norman-Meyer heeded Fanya's plea to steer clear of the lagoon. At least he did until I decided, after that discussion with Grandpa Abe about Fanya and Norman-Meyer and peace and quiet, that the Emily Park lagoon was something Norman-Meyer just *had* to see. And I figured that as long as he was going to be there anyway, why not make use of his considerable mental and physical prowess to look for the gold-plated pistol that once belonged to the notorious Baby Face Nelson?

Norman-Meyer balked at first, explaining that if he were caught, his father would hit him. I assured him that we could go to the lagoon undetected—after all, I did it all the time—and besides, I told him, "Grandpa Abe even says you should go there." That last part was not, strictly speaking, the truth, but it was close enough to it, in my mind, to suit the exigencies of the moment.

"Listen, Norman-Meyer," I said. "Don't worry. You'll love the lagoon. It's pretty and peaceful and you can hear silence there, and frogs, too. And if we find Baby Face Nelson's gun, we'll be heroes!"

Kids before me had tried to find that pistol. I always wondered whether Billy Cohen might have seen it there, under the water, in the final moments before he drowned. But nobody had located it, which only, of course, enhanced its value. So I planned my expedition conscientiously.

"Here's what we'll do," I told Norman-Meyer. "On Sunday,

when we're supposed to be going to the movies, we'll go to the lagoon instead. Nobody will know the difference. You just need to find out what film's playing at the Skokie Theater in case anybody asks any questions later on, okay? I'll handle everything else."

Norman-Meyer assented.

So at noon on the following Sunday, we were there, Norman-Meyer and I, standing at the edge of the lagoon.

My plan required a small cache of carefully selected equipment, which I'd brought along with me that day. There was my thirty-two-ounce Louisville Slugger baseball bat, autographed by Mickey Mantle. And a twelve-foot-long piece of twine, which my sister used as a jump rope. And the detached business end of a lightweight garden rake, which I'd borrowed from my father's backyard toolshed. (He wouldn't miss the rake, I figured, because it was September and the leaves hadn't really begun to fall yet, and besides, he'd be listening to the Cubs game on the radio that afternoon.) And finally, stuffed in my pocket, was a dollar—my movie money—that I gave to Ranger Fred, who ran the lagoon boathouse, in order to procure the rowboat we'd need to carry out our salvage operation. I must say that Ranger Fred did raise an eyebrow when he saw all the paraphernalia I had with me. But he was a pal, and more to the point, his girlfriend, Myrtle, was with him, and Myrtle was a looker, so he didn't pay us too much mind. "Be careful out there, boys," was all he said.

So we prepared to get under way.

Norman-Meyer had never been in a rowboat before, and he was a bit skittish at the prospect of heading out to sea.

"What if it tips over?" he asked.

"It won't," I told him. "Let's get going."

So Norman-Meyer maneuvered his hefty torso into the craft and sat down on one of the two planks, which served as seats. I handed him the tools, shoved the boat into the water, jumped in, took the oars, and pushed off.

I brought us to the bend of the lagoon, which I figured was the deepest section, and therefore the place that Baby Face Nelson's companions would most likely have deposited the firearm. Also, it was an isolated spot, hidden by a cluster of oak trees and a wall of cattails: the perfect gangster dumping ground.

"Give me the bat and the rope, Norman-Meyer," I said.

He adjusted his glasses. "I don't want to get into trouble," he said, beginning to rock himself nervously port and then starboard. The boat tilted precariously close to the water's surface with each of his weighty, anxious gestures. "And I think I'm getting seasick," he added.

"Norman-Meyer," I said, "don't be a cootie. You're not getting seasick. Stop rocking. Look, just take a deep breath and enjoy this place. Listen to the silence. It's peaceful here. And you won't get into trouble. Now just hand me the bat and the rope."

He looked up at the sky as if searching for guidance, sucked in a belly full of air, and complied with my request. I took the rope and attached one end securely to the narrow handle of the baseball bat. The ridge at the end of the bat, which I intended to use as a fishing pole, would make sure that the rope wouldn't fall off. It was a bit of engineering genius, I thought. Then, I tied the rake head to the other end of the rope, with the teeth of the rake fanning outward. The teeth would dredge the bottom of the lagoon and latch onto anything interesting, such as the trigger guard of Baby Face Nelson's pistol. Then I threw the rake into the water and watched as the weight of the device pulled the rope beneath the surface.

"Norman-Meyer," I said, "how'd you like to row a bit?"

"I don't want to get into trouble," he said.

"Don't worry, it's fun," I said. "And the exercise will do you good."

Again, a glance at the sky, a breath, and acquiescence. Norman-Meyer cautiously shifted his body into the pilot's seat, took the oars, and pummeled them at the water. At first, the boat just twisted left and right as Norman-Meyer thrashed about to control the vessel. But he was, as I've said, a smart kid, and he soon figured out how to move the boat around.

"Forward, Captain!" I said.

Norman-Meyer smiled. "Aye, aye," he said, and the craft lurched forward.

We dredged the lagoon for an hour. Norman-Meyer guided us to and fro, while I sat at the back of the boat, Louisville Slugger in hand, watching the snare I'd made trail behind in the boat's wake. I was vigilant, muscles tensed, ready to pull the rake up whenever the rope turned taut at the suggestion of having latched onto some booty. But mostly the rake just slid along the bottom, occasionally getting stuck on some lagoon undergrowth, but that's about it.

Until I felt a sharp tug at the end of the baseball bat. I jerked at the fishing line, and it seemed heavy. The rake had caught something.

I told Norman-Meyer to stop rowing, and once the boat was still, I began, ever so carefully, to pull in the rake. At first I couldn't see a thing through the brown silt of the lagoon water. But then, as I continued to draw in the rope, the sunlight hit the object beneath the surface, and gold-colored sparks of light jumped out at me through the waves. My heart started pounding.

"Norman-Meyer! Norman-Meyer!" I shouted. "Look! We caught something golden. I think it's Baby Face Nelson's gun."

Norman-Meyer let go of the oars and moved himself next to me at the back of the boat. He peered over the side as I pulled in the snare. And there, caught in the teeth of the rake, was a black velvet pouch with gold Hebrew letters embroidered on it. And I recognized the letters from my Hebrew-school lessons. And the letters spelled out *Yisgadal v'yiskadash shmey rabo*—"May his great name be magnified and sanctified." Norman-Meyer, who also understood the letters' message, looked at me, and he started to rock again, back and forth. For this was the Kaddish, the prayer for the dead. And inside the pouch was an old Jewish prayer shawl, all wet and moldy. And hand stitched onto the white face of the shawl in jagged, black-thread relief, was the word *Auschwitz*. And Norman-Meyer and I sat there quietly on the Emily Park lagoon, staring down at the water, listening to the silence.

CHAPTER 3

Auschwitz

In Skokie, everybody in the neighborhood knew where everybody else in the neighborhood was from. Abe Yellin was from Lubeshov. Reb Rappoport was from Warsaw. My parents were from Chicago. And the Singers were from Auschwitz.

Martin and Beatrice Singer lived at the end of our block, a few houses down from ours. Their daughter, Eva, went to school with Norman-Meyer and me, and on occasion, when we were feeling magnanimous, we'd even ask her to play with us. Norman-Meyer especially liked Eva, because she, like he, wore glasses. And she tended to be on the quiet side, and she never, ever teased him.

I liked Eva because she was the only girl I knew who could speak Yiddish, a skill that I much admired. Yiddish was the language my grandpa Abe spoke when he was growing up, and I wished that I could speak it, too. My parents knew Yiddish when they were children, but they lost the skill as adults, so I never had the chance to learn it. Eva, on the other hand, spoke Yiddish at home with her folks, and sometimes she'd even use it with me, which was a source of great delight.

Eva on belly buttons: "Is your *pupik* an insy or outsy, Bobby?"

Eva on cooties: "Don't tease Norman-Meyer, Bobby. You're more of a *nebbish* than he is!"

Eva after a sneeze: "*Zay gezundt*, Bobby."

Eva's parents used to live on Chicago's old West Side, and it was there that my grandpa Abe first met them. The Singers moved to the city after the war, and every Sunday, no matter what, they'd visit my grandparents' delicatessen to place an order for food.

"Mr. Yellin," Beatrice would say, "please, one pound corned beef with a half-pound slaw, and some pickled herring with lox, a quarter-pound, please. And a loaf challah. Please."

Same order. Every Sunday. Every week. For years.

Once in a while Emma, my grandmother, would invite Martin and Beatrice over for tea and cake, and the families established a friendship as a result. The Singers moved to Skokie in 1958 because they could afford a house there and they wanted Eva to go to good public schools.

It was at Eva's house one day, not long after the Singers moved to the neighborhood, that I first learned of this place called Auschwitz. Eva and I had spent the afternoon outside playing hide-and-seek with Norman-Meyer. Norman-Meyer had had a rough time of it, for he was never quite able sufficiently to hide his considerable torso behind a tree or a garbage can in order to elude capture. After we finished playing, Eva could see that Norman-Meyer was down in the dumps. "Norman-Meyer," she said sweetly, "why are you all *farklempt?*" And to lift his spirits, she invited us over to her house for chocolate milk and cookies.

We happily accepted her invitation (chocolate milk and cookies were Norman-Meyer's favorite afternoon pick-me-up), and we soon found ourselves seated at the kitchen table of Eva's home. Her mother, Beatrice, welcomed us as if we were her own, and began handing out the treats. When she reached over to put a glass down in front of me, I noticed her forearm, and the numbers that were written on it.

"Mrs. Singer, did you know that you've got numbers on your skin?" I asked.

"Yes, Bobby, I know," she said.

"She's from Auschwitz," Eva declared.

"What's Auschwitz?" I asked.

"A bad place," Eva said. "My mama and papa say it's a very bad place with really mean people."

"Now children, do not worry yourselves with such things," Beatrice said. "Please, just enjoy, enjoy, and eat your cookies and milk."

"*Mama, ken ikh zay mer zugn?*" Eva said. "Mama, can't I tell them more?"

"*Nayn, shayninke, nayn, di darfst nisht redn fin azelekhe zakhn.*" Beatrice said. "No, my pretty one, no, you mustn't speak of such things."

I remembered this kitchen conversation, sitting there in the rowboat on the Emily Park lagoon that Sunday with Norman-Meyer, trying to decipher the meaning of the black velvet pouch and the prayer shawl we'd found.

"Norman-Meyer," I said, "Eva's parents are from Auschwitz, remember?"

"I want to go home now, okay?" he said, still anxiously rocking to and fro.

"Do you think these things belong to them?" I asked. "Maybe they want them back."

"I want to go home now. Let's go home," he said.

This time I relented, and we rowed to shore, said good-bye to Ranger Fred, and headed back to our block.

I'd promised Norman-Meyer that I wouldn't tell my parents what we'd found there in the Emily Park lagoon. "If you tell your mom, she'll tell my mom, and my dad will find out, and I'll get smacked for sure," he said. But the discovery was too troubling, and too interesting, to overlook altogether. So I decided to raise the matter with Grandpa Abe, who knew about all things Jewish, who knew the Singers, and who loved me so much that he probably wouldn't tell my mother that I'd gone to Emily Park despite her instructions to the contrary.

When I showed Abe what I'd found in the lagoon, he held his heart, and sat down.

"Oy," he said.

"We were looking for Baby Face Nelson's golden revolver, Grandpa—you know, the one he had on him when he was killed?—and this is what we found instead," I said cheerfully.

"Oy," Abe repeated. "Oy, oy."

Abe took the prayer shawl with the word *Auschwitz* on it and delicately, almost reverentially, lay it down on a table to dry out. He took the black velvet pouch with the gold lettering and propped it against a shelf so it, too, could dry out. He then put on his skullcap and placed one on my head as well. He told me to be quiet, as he proceeded to recite the mourner's prayer, the Kaddish, that was embroidered on the side of the velvet pouch.

Then he told me to go home.

"But Grandpa," I protested, "I don't understand."

"Just go home," he said sternly. "And don't speak with the Singers about what you found, all right?"

I could see that Abe was genuinely upset, and I was upset that I had upset him.

"Bobby, do you hear me?" he said. "Do not tell the Singers what you found, okay? I don't want you to bother them."

"Yes, Grandpa," I said. "But why are you so troubled? I didn't mean to make you angry."

"I'm not angry at you," he said. "But these things that you've brought to my house, they're not welcome. They're from a terrible, terrible place, a place as black as black can be, and that's why I'm upset. Thank God your grandma isn't here. She'd be beside herself if she saw these things."

I lowered my eyes to the floor.

"Listen, Bobby, my grandson, you're still very young, but

you've learned enough about our ways and traditions to know that this pouch, this shawl, this Kaddish, these are sacred to us. And to find them at the bottom of a lagoon, no less. Lord knows what kind of despair drove someone to put them there."

Abe paused, let out a sigh, and picked up the prayer shawl. He stared at it, then ran his fingers over the black hand-stitched letters that spelled *Auschwitz*. He did so slowly, and thoughtfully, as if he were a blind man reading braille.

"The answer, I suspect, is found here," he said. "May you never feel one drop of the kind of pain that Auschwitz inflicted on our people. In due course, when you're older, you'll come to know what happened there, and what happened to our friends the Singers. For now I will tell you only that this prayer shawl, with this terrible word stitched into its side, carries the anguish and cries and suffering of a single Jew, and of every Jew. Now, please, just go on home. And remember, don't bother the Singers with what you found today."

I left Abe's house a sobered kid, wanting to shoot that no-good Baby Face Nelson for the trouble he'd caused me, and the anguish, through me, that he'd obviously brought to Abe. And as for this place called Auschwitz, well, the whole day's experience left me bewildered and mystified. Auschwitz was bad news, that was for sure. But I didn't really know exactly why. And I would only begin to understand the reasons later on, in Mrs. Smith's fifth-grade English class.

Mrs. Smith was the kind of teacher any parent would want their kid to have. She was just the right mix of taskmaster and nursemaid. She worked her students hard, really hard, and she expected great things from every one of us. If we put in the effort, we were rewarded with laurels of praise. "Well done, Professor!" she'd say. Or "Tremendous effort, Mr. So-and-So." It was good to receive such approbation, especially in public. But if we slacked off, or if we misbehaved, she let us know about that, too. "I'm disappointed in you." That's all she'd say. And it was enough, for that simple phrase, uttered by someone we liked so much, made us feel really bad.

Mrs. Smith taught English, and she did so with great intensity and conviction. "Reading and writing are as important in life as the very act of breathing," she'd say. "And I expect you all to be panting for breath by the time I'm through with you."

Mrs. Smith believed that the only way to learn how to read was to read, and the only way to learn how to write was to write. A lot. Endurance training for the mind, she'd say. The more you do it, the better you get at it, and the better you get at it, the more you like it. Her reading assignments brought us to places and language and syntax we'd never seen before. *Huckleberry Finn, A Midsummer Night's Dream,* the poetry of e. e. cummings. Heavy lifting for fifth-grade eyes. As for writing, her single-minded intent was to breed for the world a new crop of young Shakespeares. Nothing more. Nothing less. So it was with that lofty goal in mind that each Monday and Tuesday and Wednesday and Thursday and Friday, at the end of class, Mrs. Smith would give us a writing assignment to work on at home.

"Young Shakespeares," Mrs. Smith said one day, "I want you to write an essay about someone you admire. I want you to write about someone who's not in your family, if you can, because writing about your mother or father is a little too easy, I think. What I'd like you to do is to think hard and broaden your horizons. Try to come up with someone else. And once you've selected someone, tell me why this person has earned your respect, and what it is about him that you admire. I want one or two pages. Quality is important, not quantity. And be prepared to read your essay out loud in class. The assignment is due tomorrow."

I still have that essay, after all these years, along with all the others I wrote for Mrs. Smith. They're in an old, yellowed folder with a scrawled, fountain-penned label that reads: "My Writings for Mrs. Helen Smith." It's a memorial, of sorts, to a teacher who made a difference. And the essay, which I can reproduce here, verbatim, pays indirect homage to my grandpa, whose way with words I especially admired. It reads as follows:

THE PERSON NOT IN MY FAMILY WHO I ADMIRE
by Bobby Bakalchuk:

Eenie, meanie, mynie, moe-it,
I admire most the Poet.
Only he would take the time
To make of words a verse, a rhyme.

Eenie, meanie, mynie, me-zee,
Rhyming words is awfully easy,
Making verses so delicious
Like my Grandma Emma's knishes.

Eenie, meanie, mynie, myew-ish,
Poetry can rhyme in Jewish.
Just don't make your poems too chipper
When you're fasting on Yom Kippur.

Eenie, meanie, mynie moe-key,
Words can even rhyme with Skokie.
Rhyming words that is my hobby,
Good thing that my name is Bobby.

Eenie, meanie, mynie, marrow,
Poems can be fat, long or narrow,
Poems can rock n' roll, especially
When they're sung by Elvis Presley.

Eenie, meanie, mynie, moe-ver,
Guess it's time this poem were over.
There's no doubt, now you all know it,
I admire most: the Poet.

After I read my essay in verse in front of the class, Mrs. Smith applauded and said, "Wonderful. Wonderful. We'll make a Shakespeare out of you yet, Bobby. Well done." I thrived on Mrs. Smith's approval, and her reaction made me feel very proud. It was, quite simply, the highlight of my grammar school career, such as it was until that point in time.

Mrs. Smith then called on Ronnie Schwab, who said he admired Big Herm, the well-known fast food concessionaire, because Herm was a fine businessman who put extra relish and onions on his hot dogs. Then Norman-Meyer trudged to the front of the class and read an essay in praise of Chaim and Mort, his pet parrots. "I think of them as people," Norman-Meyer said, "and I admire them as such." Then Myron Kaufmann stood up and said he admired Mrs. Smith. (Myron was a suck-up.) Then Kristina O'Brien, who said she admired the pope. And Tommy Greenstein, who said the only thing he admired was his brother's car and maybe Solly, the local auto mechanic. At age eleven, Tommy, we presumed, was well on his way to becoming a Jewish mobster.

Then it was Eva's turn. I thought perhaps she might name me as the object of her admiration, since I'd recently taught her how to stick four fingers into her mouth and whistle.

I was wrong.

"My mama and papa are the only people in the whole world that I admire," Eva said. "And I wish that I could make all my admiration turn into gold, because then my parents would be rich, because I have so much admiration for them. Or maybe it would be better if admiration were some sort of medicine pill, because then my mama and papa could take it, and maybe their bad dreams would go away, and maybe they'd smile and laugh a little bit more.

"My mama and papa tell me not to talk about what happened to them before I was born. They say it was a long time ago, and it's something that should remain in the family. But I can see that the memory of what happened is still with them today, and I think that maybe if I write about it, maybe they'll be able to write about it too, so other people will know, and maybe they'll feel better.

"I ask my mama and papa to tell me the stories at night, while I lay in bed, warm and safe under the covers. 'Papa,' I say, 'please tell me what happened to your sister.' Or 'Mama,' I say, 'please tell me what happened to my grandma and grandpa.' They really don't want to, but I beg them and beg them to tell me, because I love them, and I want to know what happened to them so maybe I can make them feel better. And they tell me about an evil man named Hitler who lived in Germany and wanted to kill every single Jewish person he could find. He found my parents, and all of their family and friends, and he sent them to a terrible place called Auschwitz. Hitler killed most of them there. My grandma Eve died there. My grandpas, Aaron and Joshua, died there too, and so did Uncle Pinchas and Uncle Hymie and Aunty Klara. I never met my relatives, but my mama and papa have told me all about them, and I think I would have admired them. Especially my grandma Eve, who had green eyes, like me. I was named after Grandma Eve.

"My mama and papa managed to survive the place called Auschwitz. Papa says he doesn't know why or how. It was God's will, he says. Papa says he would rather have died there than to have buried his own brother and sister, or to have watched what the bad people there did to my mama. When I ask my mama what happened, she tells me not to worry, and turns away. I know she's crying, even though she tries to hide it. And I start to cry too, because I know they must have hurt her real bad.

"So I admire my mama and papa because of what they went through, and because they try to live as best they can with the memory of the terrible things that happened to them there at that place they call Auschwitz. And I admire them because they have the strength to tell me about that place, even though it must be difficult. I just wish they could tell other people, too. Because I think that other people ought to know."

Eva said Martin and Beatrice were furious when they'd learned about the essay she'd written and read to the class. They found out from Mrs. Smith, who'd been so touched and surprised by Eva's story that she'd felt compelled to call the Singers.

"Mrs. Smith told my mama and papa that she admires them, and asked if there was anything she could do," Eva said. "My parents said no, thank you, and they told Mrs. Smith that they don't seek admiration and they don't need anybody's help. And they apologized to Mrs. Smith for any trouble I may have caused her, and when they got off the phone they yelled at me."

"Mir hobn dir gezugt zolst kaynmul nisht tse redn vegn di zakhn mit fremde! We told you never to speak of such things to outsiders!" Martin Singer told his daughter. "Don't you listen?" he said. "Nobody can understand what we went through unless they went through it themselves, and to speak of it only invites pity. *Men vet af ins nisht rakhmones hobn, Eva. Naynmul mer nisht.* And we will not be pitied, Eva, never again."

Outsiders. I don't imagine there's a better way to describe how the Singers saw the rest of the world, and their own place in it. They belonged to a clan that was formed in the death camps, and whose language derived from an experience so tragic that only they and others like them could speak it. Those who couldn't they considered *fremde,* outsiders. Yet Martin and Beatrice Singer regarded themselves as outsiders, too, even in Skokie, among the American-born Jews there, who treated them kindly and with respect, but who knew they were different.

"My parents always felt like greenhorns," Eva once told me years later. "They were always 'the survivors,' those poor people who spoke with accents, and they never felt accepted by American Jews, even in Skokie. So they felt insecure. And they stayed with their own."

And they did the best they could, with their own, for there were many like them in Skokie. They embraced each other, and together, they embraced suburban life, cherishing the houses they'd managed to buy, which were mansions of prosperity, calm, and security compared with the camps they once called home. And they socialized, almost always among themselves: survivor group picnics, summertime survivor outings to the Lake Michigan beachfront, even survivor bowling leagues. And, of course, they bore children, and raised them to be Jews, thereby replenishing the stock that Hitler had taken away from them.

And some of the families, like the Singers, told their children about Auschwitz, or Dachau, or Treblinka, and about what happened there. But there were others who didn't, who couldn't bear to burden their small sons and daughters with such *tsures*, with such grief.

In high school, Eva told me a story about her friend Rachel, who was also a daughter of survivors. Eva and Rachel went to the Skokie Theater to see *Judgment at Nuremberg*, the film about the Nazi war-crime trials. It was the first time Rachel had learned the horrible details of her parents' wartime experience. "Rachel went home enraged," Eva said. "She told her mother and father that she would never forgive them for not telling her the whole truth about what had happened to them. She hated finding out that way, at the movies. And her parents felt terrible, but all they could say to her was, 'Forgive us, but we couldn't tell you about it. It was too painful, and we didn't want to hurt you.'"

But Rachel's parents spoke about their pain with Martin and Beatrice. And Martin and Beatrice spoke about the Holocaust with their survivor friends. Among the survivors, such talk was common, even encouraged. It was a way, the only way, really, to heal, to mend. But to speak with outsiders, as Eva found out, was something different. And that wouldn't begin to change until 1967, when Israel defeated the Arabs in the Six-Day War.

For the survivors who lived in Skokie, a straight line ran from Israel back to the Holocaust. A direct and vital link. Israel was *their* country, given to them as compensation for all they had gone through. It was through mere happenstance that they found themselves living in the United States. They would rather have been in Israel, and the bond they felt to the Jewish state was unyielding.

"Israel was everything to us," Martin Singer told me. "It meant a lot to any Jew, yes, but to us, it was something different. Israel represented for us life itself, and we would give all our lives for it. It was the soul of Judaism that Hitler had tried to burn out but couldn't. And when Israel was victorious in 1967, when this tiny state won against all odds, we found it empowering. We got encouraged, and it somehow gave us a sense of security that we had never felt since the Nazis. We could finally pick our heads up and go high."

When the Six-Day War began in June 1967, life as we knew it in Skokie stopped. Israel's war was our war, and even during the school day, nobody could think or speak of anything else. Television sets ran around the clock, even in our classrooms, and we'd sit there in front of the screen, looking at maps of Israel and Jordan and Syria and Egypt, following along as Walter Cronkite described Israeli troop movements here and there across the Sinai, West Bank, Golan Heights, and, miraculously, into the

Old City of Jerusalem. And we'd cheer and clap when Israel's boys did well, as if our team had just scored a touchdown. And we sat silently when things looked bad.

Beatrice Singer happened to be visiting a cousin in New York City when the war broke out. So Martin was home alone with Eva when my grandpa Abe came knocking at their door.

"Abe was organizing an emergency fund-raising drive for Israel, and he knew us, so he came over and asked for some money," Martin said. "And I had saved up five hundred dollars. It was all we had in savings, you know, money we were putting away for Eva for college. And I asked Abe, I said Abe, can you tell me what you are expecting? And he said whatever I could afford. And I said we've got five hundred dollars; do you think this is enough? I'll tell you, that was our fortune. That's all we had. And I gave away my last penny to Abe, and he was astounded. He said nobody, nobody, had been as generous as me. And then, afterwards, I thought, oy, what about Beatrice, what will she think when she gets back home? And she came back from New York and I picked her up at the train station, and I said, Beatrice, I have to tell you something and I hope you won't be mad. So, you know the five hundred dollars we have saved up? I gave it away for the emergency fund for Israel. And she smiled and said 'God bless you, Martin Singer, for what you have done, but such a cheapskate you are. You couldn't give more?' And she kissed me and said money is just money, there will always be that. But Israel is Israel, and we must do what we can to help her."

And after the war was over, after Israel had won, Martin and some of his survivor friends decided to take a stand. They had lived as greenhorns long enough, they said. It was time to assert themselves, like Israel; time to make a mark on the community; time to affirm their identity in an organized fashion. And time, maybe, to think about sharing their stories with outsiders, so nobody would forget what had happened to them.

So they set to the task. With phone calls, with coffees, with lox and bagels and vodka and cajoling and even a little bit of arm twisting, they created an association of Holocaust survivors in Skokie. They named the group after Janusz Korczak, a Polish physician who cared for the children of the Warsaw ghetto. Korczak was murdered in the camps, having refused to abandon his children, even though, had he done so, the Germans would have set him free. Martin Singer had watched as Korczak, along with his two hundred kids, walked to their deaths.

The Korczak Unit, as the association was called, became a fund-raising organization, donating money to Israel and to a variety of other Jewish causes. During the 1973 Arab-Israeli War, the group even sent two of its members, who were physicians, to Tel Aviv, where they delivered a sizable check, and worked in a children's hospital, freeing up local staff for combat duty.

Members of the organization also began, cautiously at first, to appear in public, answering questions at schools and at synagogues about their experiences during the Holocaust. The more they did it, the more they realized that it made them feel good.

By the time the American Nazi Frank Collin announced his intention to march into Skokie, the Korczak Unit had become a well-oiled and politically potent player in Skokie affairs, with a membership of nearly seven thousand. So nobody was surprised, after my grandpa's arrest, when Martin Singer, the unit's president, telephoned his old friend Abe and announced the establishment of the Abe Yellin Legal Action Fund. The objective, said Martin, was to keep Frank Collin and his storm troopers out of Skokie. And Abe Yellin's case would be the focal point of a court effort to do just that.

CHAPTER 4

The First Amendment

Frank Collin had been a busy Nazi in the months since Abe Yellin, with his kosher salami, had stood his ground on the village ramparts and beaten back the storm trooper's attempt to enter Skokie. Collin had produced a flyer, which circulated widely in the community, proclaiming his plan to hold a Nazi rally there no matter what. "We Are Coming!" the flyer declared. "Smash the Jewish System!" it added. The flyer said Collin had selected Skokie because "where one finds the most Jews, there one finds the most Jew-haters." The flyer also displayed a big, black swastika, and a crude, beak-nosed caricature of a Jewish man.

Collin had also unleashed some artfully penned political doggerel, with assistance from the press. His "manifesto" on the Skokie controversy was published, free of charge, in one of the big Chicago newspapers. Thanks to that editorial action, the piece was read in nearly every Jewish household in the greater metropolitan area, chilling more than a few spines.

"We want to reach the good people in Skokie," Collin wrote.

We want to get the fierce anti-Semites who have to live among the Jews to come out of the woodwork and stand up for themselves. I hope the survivors are terrified. I hope they're shocked. Because we're coming to get them again. I don't care if someone's mother or father or brother died in the gas chambers. The unfortunate thing is not that there were six million Jews who died. The unfortunate thing is that there were so many Jewish survivors.

Then there were the phone calls. In the middle of the night. First to Abe Yellin. Then to Martin Singer. Then, randomly, to any Skokie resident listed in the phone book whose name was obviously Jewish. The Steins got one. So did the various Cohens. Old man Weiss was honored. And dozens more. The messages carried the same theme: "Die Jew." "Kill the kikes." "The ovens are too good for you." The Skokie police could never trace the calls to Collin or members of his Nazi band. But no matter. Everyone knew where they came from.

And, finally, this bit of news, reported in the *Chicago Sun-Times*: a Chicago man claiming to be a Nazi follower was arrested for murdering a Jew by forcing him to inhale hydrogen cyanide. Hydrogen cyanide was the essential component of Zyklon B, the poisonous gas used by Hitler in the Nazi death camps. Collin vehemently disavowed any connection to the affair, saying he didn't want to kill the Jews, he just wanted to deport them. And the perpetrator admitted he'd never met Collin. But the incident, and the horrible nature of the crime, further set Skokie on edge.

That suited Frank Collin just fine. But it made Steven Klein's ulcer burn just a bit brighter, as if it needed additional tinder.

Klein was a lawyer. Lead counsel for the Chicago branch of the American Civil Liberties Union (ACLU). The ACLU was in the business of defending the First Amendment. Whenever the government tried to censor the views of someone it disliked, the ACLU was there. Its clients were often unpopular, and sometimes outright disgusting. The Nazis, and Frank Collin in particular, had never been shy about asking the ACLU to intervene on their behalf—all in the name of the Constitution, of course. Steven Klein, in fact, had represented Collin once before, when the City of Chicago had tried to block a Nazi demonstration in Marquette Park. So it was Klein whom Collin telephoned when the people of Skokie decided they didn't want brownshirts and jackboots soiling the streets and sidewalks of their village.

Klein was a principled man who at age fifty had served the ACLU for nearly twenty years. His curly gray hair and horn-rimmed glasses gave him a soft, professorial appearance that belied a sharp tongue and an unwavering, steel-like determination to protect the Bill of Rights. Klein had four passions in life: his wife, his daughter, the Chicago Cubs, and the First Amendment. There were times when his wife complained that the First Amendment was Klein's first love, and not she. A framed text of the amendment hung on the wall over their bed. And when Klein's child was young, she didn't recite the Lord's Prayer before settling down for the night. At Klein's instruction, she exhorted the Constitution: "God bless Mommy and Daddy and this great country, where Congress shall make no law abridging freedom of speech or of the press."

Klein traced his affection for the First Amendment to 1948, and an incident involving his father, Milton Klein. Milton was a labor organizer for the United Packinghouse Workers Union in Chicago. Like many labor activists of the time, Milton belonged to the Communist Party. In 1947, with the cold war well under way, the United States Congress passed the Taft-Hartley Act, which required union officials to sign affidavits disavowing any and all Communist affiliations. Failure to do so carried a heavy sanction: the government could strip away a union's official certification, effectively putting it out of business. Milton and many of his union colleagues refused to sign on, claiming the

Taft-Hartley Act violated their free speech rights under the First Amendment. They filed suit in Federal District Court challenging the law. In March 1948, with the litigation still unsettled, the Chicago police raided one of the Packinghouse Workers Union shops in an effort to weed out Communist sympathizers. Milton, who was on the scene, verbally protested the police action. An overzealous cop, shouting "Get yer dirty Red ass back to Moscow," busted Milton's head open. Milton Klein was never the same again. And Steven, who spent the next two weeks at his father's hospital bedside, resolved, in the name of his battered parent, to do all he could from that point on to make sure nobody else's head got bashed in for speaking his mind.

Steven's First Amendment field training took place in the South during the 1960s. He was one of a dozen or so ACLU attorneys affiliated with the Lawyers Constitutional Defense Committee, which helped black civil rights leaders secure, through the courts, whatever legal advantage they could. There was no shortage of work to be done back then, and Klein was involved in scores of cases. He represented blacks who were arrested for using a Louisiana bus depot's "whites only" waiting room; he defended civil rights activists who were jailed for holding a peaceful sit-in at a segregated Mississippi public library. And, most prominently, there was the case of the Reverend Fred L. Shuttlesworth, of Birmingham, Alabama. Klein and his colleagues brought that one all the way to the United States Supreme Court.

Shuttlesworth was a prominent African American minister who'd been arrested for leading a peaceful civil rights procession on the sidewalks of Birmingham in 1963. Shuttlesworth staged the march without a permit. He was convicted of violating a city ordinance that gave officials broad power to block public demonstrations on the basis of "public welfare, peace, safety, health, decency, good order, morals or convenience."

The Supreme Court struck down the law, saying it put into the hands of Birmingham officials unbridled authority to abridge a citizen's right to speak out against the government.

Klein remembered Birmingham when Frank Collin called him to talk about Skokie. Collin was no Reverend Shuttlesworth, and his cause was as unappealing as Shuttlesworth's was just. But in Klein's view, the First Amendment belonged to everyone, even to a sleazy character like Collin. And Klein knew that Skokie's effort to stop the Nazi rally was unconstitutional on its face. It smacked of Birmingham. So Klein took Collin's case.

At issue were the three Skokie ordinances specifically tailored to suppress Collin's speech by keeping him out of the village. One banned the dissemination of material in Skokie that "promotes and incites hatred against persons by reason of their race, national origin, or religion." The second prohibited public demonstrations by members of political parties wearing military-style uniforms. And the third required parade permit applicants to obtain $350,000 in liability and property damage insurance. No insurance, no permit.

"Your Honor," Klein said in the first court hearing challenging the ordinances, "if this Court issues a preliminary injunction in this case, enjoining the demonstration of Mr. Collin and the National Socialist Party of America, I fear that the Village of Skokie will be dancing on the grave of the First Amendment."

Initially, Klein's eloquence got him nowhere. A series of local judges blocked the Nazi rally outright. One even did so surreptitiously at a hearing that neither Klein nor Collin attended. The actions pleased Skokie's Jewish residents, but enraged Klein, who saw the whole thing as dangerous political theater acted out by a bunch of popularly elected courtroom political hacks who lived for reelection and cared little about the law.

Eventually, however, the Supreme Court of the United States

stepped in. On June 14, 1977, the justices ruled that the Illinois courts had denied Frank Collin the "strict procedural safeguards" the Constitution required when First Amendment rights were at issue. In other words, in the opinion of the nation's high court, the Illinois courts had screwed up. In their zeal to censor Collin, they'd deprived him of a timely, fair, and impartial hearing. Until such a hearing was held, the Supreme Court said, the Nazis and Frank Collin were free to march in Skokie.

Steven Klein was delighted with the decision. Abe Yellin and Martin Singer were not. The village had let them down. Not only had Skokie lawyers failed to block plans for Collin's march, but they had somehow allowed the United States Supreme Court to stick its judicial nose into the mess. "What do you expect?" Abe Yellin said of the high court's adverse decision. "There isn't a Jew among them."

After the Supreme Court's action, the Abe Yellin Legal Action Fund and Norman-Meyer Ashkenaz took over. Norman-Meyer had blossomed in the years since our childhood, at least as a student. He'd excelled in high school and in college, drinking in advanced placement courses with the same abandon and gusto with which he imbibed chocolate milk shakes, root beer floats, and other favorite libations. His grades rode high along with his weight, and he earned valedictory honors wherever he went. After college, Norman-Meyer won a full scholarship to Yale Law School. In his second year there he became deputy editor of the *Yale Law Journal,* where he did some groundbreaking work on the law against perpetuities. His academic adviser, Professor Pock, said Norman-Meyer was "as sharp in mind as he is slovenly in appearance."

Norman-Meyer graduated from Yale in 1974 in the top 3 percent of his class. He came back home to Skokie afterward ("I just fit in better there," he wrote me), took up residence in his parents' house (his father, Joseph, agreed to give him his old room back in return for free legal assistance upon demand), and got a job with a big Chicago law firm.

So, when Martin Singer asked Norman-Meyer to volunteer as chief counsel for the Abe Yellin Legal Action Fund, the young lawyer was ready to go. He puffed up his chest, stroked the goatee he'd grown to cover an ever expanding double chin, shook Martin's hand, and declared, with evident delight, that he would proudly serve in that capacity.

"So, Mr. Lawyer, what will you do?" Martin Singer asked him.

"*Chaplinsky,*" Norman-Meyer replied.

The free speech provisions of the First Amendment are nearly impervious. They are a fire wall designed to ward off any assault against the nation's most fundamental liberty interest: the freedom to speak your mind without fear of reprisal. Norman-Meyer knew that as well as Steven Klein. Two hundred years of American jurisprudence had shown that U.S. citizens, Nazis included, could pretty much say what they wanted, and, at least with respect to political speech, there wasn't much anybody could do about it. The framers of the Bill of Rights figured that the country needed to hear extreme discourse from time to time in order to prosper. The nation is a marketplace of ideas, they said, and the government has no role in controlling what enters the stream of ideological commerce. If someone says something abhorrent, let the power of opposing points of view provide the counterweight, not government censorship.

But there were some small exceptions to the rule, and Norman-Meyer knew that *Chaplinsky* was one of them.

He had read the case, formally known as *Chaplinsky vs. the State of New Hampshire,* in his constitutional law class at Yale. The Court's opinion fascinated Norman-Meyer because, to his mind, it involved the rights of people, like himself, who'd been victimized by verbal taunts and abuse. He sometimes good-naturedly called *Chaplinsky* the "cootie case."

In *Chaplinsky*, the defendant, a Mr. Chaplinsky, was held criminally liable in state court for angrily and maliciously calling a couple of upstanding government officials "damned Fascists" and "damned racketeers." He might as well have told them their mothers smelled like Mussolini's armpit, for it was 1942, the height of the Second World War, and such epithets were considered inflammatory and incriminating "fighting words" under New Hampshire law, particularly when directed against honorable public servants. The Supreme Court had little patience for Chaplinsky's behavior, and it upheld his conviction.

Norman-Meyer found the outcome pleasing. In his view, the case had a broad reach, and should be applied to any well-meaning citizen targeted by inappropriately hostile and harmful rhetoric. Foul-mouthed jerks like Chaplinsky, jerks who torment and abuse people they don't like, well, they should get what's coming to them, Norman-Meyer thought. If only *he* could have used *Chaplinsky* to offset his father's belligerent and mean-spirited tongue. If only *he* could have used *Chaplinsky* against the legions of kids who had teased him incessantly while he was growing up. *Chaplinsky*, Norman-Meyer figured, was well written to protect decent people from the type of emotional harm that he had experienced throughout his lifetime. And it could be used, he reckoned, to shield the people of Skokie from the trauma they'd suffer if Frank Collin and his Nazi cronies came to town.

Norman-Meyer reread the case, first once, and then again, and then again. And he memorized—for that's what a good lawyer does—the opinion's key language. Then he summoned Martin Singer and Abe Yellin, sat them down, and proceeded to recite from memory what he'd learned.

"Gentlemen," Norman-Meyer said—he was clearly relishing

the soapbox these two respected elders of the community had given him—"Gentlemen, I'd like you to listen carefully to the words I'm about to utter, because I think they can help us. They come from a United States Supreme Court case called *Chaplinsky vs. the State of New Hampshire.* If you wish, you can find the opinion at 315 U.S. 568."

Martin and Abe looked at each other. They had no idea what "315 U.S. 568" meant, but they were impressed that Norman-Meyer knew. "Good school, Yale," Martin whispered. "Must be Jews in charge, eh, Abe?"

Norman-Meyer continued. "In *Chaplinsky,* the Supreme Court of the United States said, and I quote: 'It is well understood that the right of free speech is *not absolute* at all times and under all circumstances. There are certain well-defined and narrowly limited classes of speech, the *prevention* and *punishment* of which have *never* been thought to raise any constitutional problem.' "

Norman-Meyer verbally punched the key words of the decision with a staccato-like emphasis so that Martin and Abe would understand fully.

"These limited classes of speech 'include the lewd and obscene, the profane, the libelous, and the insulting or *fighting words*—those which by their *very utterance* inflict injury or tend to incite an immediate *breach of the peace.* It has been well observed that such utterances are no essential part of any exposition of ideas, and are of such *slight social value* as a step to truth that any benefit that may be derived from them is *clearly outweighed* by the social interest in *order* and *morality.*' "

"Gentlemen, here's what we're going to do," Norman-Meyer said, punching the air with a clenched fist to underline his point. The jab upset his tortoise-shell glasses, which fell to the end of his nose and hung there like Spanish moss. Norman-Meyer paused and stared cross-eyed down at his runaway spectacles.

He blushed for a moment, then self-consciously pushed them back into place.

"Gentlemen," he continued, "we're going to have Abe Yellin go to court and say that Frank Collin and the Nazis can't come to Skokie because their reprehensible message is the legal equivalent of fighting words. The courts, in cases since *Chaplinsky*, have defined 'fighting words,' and I quote, as 'utterances or *symbols* so personally insulting and cruel that they're inherently likely to provoke a violent reaction.' We'll argue that the swastika is such a symbol, and that its display in Skokie, in a small community like ours with tens of thousands of Jews and thousands of Holocaust survivors, is constitutionally unprotected; that to display the swastika here is to utter fighting words that are immoral and cruel and reprehensible and totally without any redeeming social value, and totally outside the reach of the First Amendment; and that to display the swastika here would produce such trauma as to almost certainly provoke violence. I mean, it already has. Abe, when you threw that salami at Frank Collin, you went and proved our case! You, the kindest, most gentle man I've ever met, a scholar and a poet, you took one look at the swastika on that Nazi's armband and you lost it. If that's not fighting words, I don't know what is!"

Beads of perspiration covered Norman-Meyer's brow, so zealous had his presentation been. Martin Singer slapped him on the back—dislodging, again, his tortoise-shell glasses—gave him a hearty *mazel tov*, and said that this "salami defense" of his (that's what Martin called it) just might work. He told Norman-Meyer to focus all his attention on the preparation of the court documents they'd need for the case of *Yellin vs. Collin*. Meantime, Martin said, he and Abe would work in the court of public opinion.

"Abe, my dear friend," Martin said, "I think it's time to go to shul." They packed up their things, bid Norman-Meyer farewell, and headed down to Temple Shalom, where they set into motion plans for a public debate on the Skokie affair that would make headlines around the world and nearly rip Steven Klein's ulcer apart.

I'd kept up with the controversy involving my grandpa, the Nazis, and Skokie from Munich, where, you'll recall, I was living and working at the time. I spoke with Abe by phone at least once a week. And the *Suddeutsche Zeitung*, southern Germany's premier daily newspaper, provided full and sometimes daily coverage. The newspaper's editors had even rented a small flat near the Skokie Village Hall to facilitate the work of the special correspondent they'd assigned to report on the story full-time. Clearly, modern postwar Germany was fascinated by the events in my hometown, and readers couldn't get enough news about the Americans and *"their* Nazis."

When Abe told me about the gathering planned at Temple Shalom, I decided it was time to come home for a visit. The event, which Martin Singer and the Korczak Unit had orchestrated, was billed as a "public forum on the Nazi threat." For the first time since the dispute had erupted, the opposing sides would meet together, in one place and in plain view of village citizens, to discuss the issues and to hear public comment. Steven Klein of the ACLU had agreed to speak on behalf of Frank Collin (or, as Klein preferred to put it, "on behalf of the First Amendment"). And Martin Singer and my grandfather would represent the Jews of Skokie.

Abe was waiting for me at O'Hare Airport when my flight from Munich, via New York, touched down in Chicago. We hugged, and Grandma Emma, who was also there, began to cry. Abe didn't say much as we made our way to the baggage claim area. He stood there next to me, holding my hand, smiling, content to have his grandson by his side for the ordeal ahead.

"Grandpa, you've lost a little weight," I said.

"And you've put on a few pounds," he replied, poking at my midsection with his finger.

"Yeah. Too much beer and apple strudel," I said. "Are you doing okay?"

"Yes, yes, I'm fine," he said. "Just fine."

Emma shot me a look that suggested otherwise. "Bobby, this has been a burden on your grandfather, a huge burden for a man of his age to carry."

"Emma, my darling, beautiful bride, respect the elders among us, for you too are bound to get old," Abe said.

Emma smiled and kissed her husband. "Always an answer he has," she said. "But Abe, it goes on, day in and day out, without letup. The meetings. The telephone calls. The interviews. And now, the lawyers. I don't see an end to it. And I worry about you."

"It must be done," Abe said. "They will not come to Skokie. Never. I don't care what the courts say, even the Supreme Court. In the name of my dead sister, Mary, who died at the hands of the Nazis simply because she was a Jew, they will not come. And look, now, who opposes us. This Klein person, Steven Klein, a Jew no less, is defending them. A Jew standing up for a Nazi! History teaches, but some never learn. May he burn in hell along with that snake, Collin. Now, Bobby, you must be hungry. Let's go home."

Abe spent the next week in seclusion, preparing for the Temple Shalom forum, which was scheduled eight days thence. At least once a day, Martin Singer would come by, and the two men, like old warriors, would huddle, arm in arm, pouring over press clippings as if they were battle maps, talking tactics and strategies, boosting each other's morale, and praying.

I was assigned the task of getting the press to cover the gathering, but there wasn't much work to be done on that score.

Journalists from all over the globe were already descending on Skokie to report on the forum. The *New York Times* was sending a reporter. So were the *Washington Post* and the *Los Angeles Times*. Paris's *Le Monde* sent somebody, as did the *Times* of London and Manchester's *Guardian*. The resident *Suddeutsche Zeitung* reporter had to order extra cots for his apartment to accommodate German colleagues from the *Frankfurter Allgemeine Zeitung* and German television. Even *Pravda*, the Soviet newspaper, had ordered its Washington correspondent to go to Skokie, but the State Department, angered at Moscow's human rights policies, refused to issue a travel visa. "Gestapo Tactics in America Block Press Coverage of Nazi March," the sanctimoniously peeved *Pravda* reporter wrote.

By the time the forum opened, Temple Shalom resembled a convention hall as much as a place of worship. A mini press center had been set up at the rear of the synagogue's main sanctuary, complete with rigs for television lights and a bank of telephones. Special seating areas were cordoned off for honored delegations: Skokie government officials, the Chamber of Commerce, local church representatives, and the Temple Shalom Save Soviet Jewry Committee. As for the general audience, the temple had never seen such a crowd, not even on the high holidays. One thousand Skokie residents, many of them survivors, filled the synagogue's main chamber.

I decided to watch the affair from backstage, along with Norman-Meyer and Eva Singer, who'd also come home for the forum. Eva was a graduate student in the Department of Jewish Studies at Columbia University, where she was writing a dissertation on Yiddish literature of the Holocaust. "I'm so proud of my father and your grandfather for what they're doing," she said. "I had to be here for this. *Men volt mikh nisht gekent tsirikhaltn, far kayn shim gelt!* No amount of money could have kept me away!"

At the front of the sanctuary, facing the crowd, with the Holy Ark containing the scrolls of the Torah as a backdrop, sat Martin Singer, Abe Yellin, Steven Klein, and Sidney Glickman—Temple Shalom's rabbi, who served as moderator.

Steven Klein had barely made it to the meeting that evening. Simply put, his wife didn't want him to attend. Klein had received a death threat the night before from a caller who said, "If you come to Skokie, you son-of-a-bitch turncoat, you won't go home." Klein dismissed the call, but his wife had informed the Skokie police, and they took the matter seriously. It was only after the village police chief insisted on providing Steven Klein with an armed escort that Klein's wife relented and allowed her husband to venture out. Just to be safe, the police made Klein enter the temple through a rear basement door.

Rabbi Glickman opened the forum. "The anti-Nazi side will go first," he said. Then he looked at Steven Klein. "And the Nazi supporter will go second. Then we'll take questions from the audience."

At Martin's urging, Abe had agreed to speak for the both of them on behalf of the Jews of Skokie. Grandpa fashioned himself as an awkward public speaker, and, after Rabbi Glickman introduced him, he seemed to struggle a bit as he walked, slightly stooped, to the lectern. As Abe was making his way to the microphone, people sitting in the audience began to rise, a group here, a group there, until the entire congregation was on its feet. They did not applaud. Rather, they stood silently, in a powerful show of respect and admiration for my grandfather.

"Please, please, my friends, sit down, sit down," Abe said. "Please don't embarrass me."

"SALAMI!" someone shouted from the crowd, breaking the silence. And everyone burst into laughter and applause.

Abe grinned, and steadied himself against the lectern. It was time to begin.

"Listen, my dear friends, I must apologize to you, for I am forever sorry and regretful that I wasn't born with the power of speech," Abe said. "I hope I won't bore you this evening. You know, I've always admired dynamic speakers, like our Rabbi Glickman here. And I have heard that this man, this Mr. Steven Klein, this Jew who defends the Nazis, I have heard that he, too, has a gifted tongue. I am envious of such people. They have the skill to express their beliefs and convictions to the degree of gaining adherents to their various points of view, even if they are wrong. I'm afraid that I lack such skills. But I will do the best I can tonight to tell you what weighs on my mind.

"As I stand before you here, and before this Torah behind me, I recall the words of our sages: '*Da meayin boso, lifnai mi ato omed, ulean ato holech.* Know where you came from, know before whom you stand, and know where you are going.' We must realize, my friends, who we are, that we were born Jews, and we will die as Jews. We must let the world, before whom we stand, know what we stand for, and that is righteousness and justice. And we must know that wherever we head, we must head there with our eyes open, and with our minds and bodies unshackled by apathy.

"History teaches," Abe said. "And we Jews have learned the price of apathy and inaction. The peoples of the world were unconcerned about the plight of our brethren in Europe. They felt secure in their positions and were apathetic to rumors of genocide. Even some Jews chose to close their eyes and ears. If only they had acted. If only *we* had acted more forcefully. The State of Israel did not have to be molded in a crematorium, like some iron put through fire in order to fashion an ornament. Oh, what a high price we paid for our complacency!

"There are those who say that complacency is not the issue here today, that there is no threat before which to be complacent, that our village is secure, that this is not Nazi Germany, that this is America, that one crazy man with his crazy ideas cannot threaten our way of life. And I say that those who say that are wrong. In Germany, Hitler was not faced early. That was the lesson of the Holocaust. Never again shall we Jews make that mistake.

"I say to you that the nightmare will not recur. The Nazis will not come here to our village. They will not wave the swastika in front of our eyes, and in front of the eyes of our children. There are among us at this very moment hundreds of survivors who suffered in ways that are unimaginable. These people, and others less blessed, like me, lost entire families to the Nazis. Lost mothers. Lost fathers. Lost siblings, like my beloved sister, Mary. Lost children. We, all of us who have been touched by the Holocaust, have promised the dead that the swastika will never again appear among us. And we will do whatever it takes to honor that promise.

"No First Amendment can change that. No First Amendment can embrace the Nazi swastika. The Nazis would destroy the very democracy that allows them to exist. On what basis, then, do they deserve to be protected by the fruits of that democracy? The filth that they propagate is repugnant. Thoroughly repugnant. And no civilized society should make room for it. And their leader, this snake who spit at my feet, this Frank Collin, is a monster. He wants to come here to hurt us. And I say if he comes here, we will hurt him. There will be victims, and the victims will not be us."

Abe then turned to Steven Klein, and spoke to him directly.

"There's a saying in the Talmud, Mr. Klein. 'Al tiftach peb l'satan.' It means 'Don't feed propaganda to the enemy.' Isn't it paradoxical that the American Civil Liberties Union is defending the rights of the Nazis, who would, if given the opportunity, quickly take away everyone else's rights, and most assuredly the rights of Jewish lawyers, like you, who are working for the

ACLU? What you're doing, Mr. Klein, is it not an insult to the memory of six million Jews, six million of your own people? Have you no respect for the rights of the survivors who sit before you? Shame on you, Mr. Klein. Shame on you. May God have mercy on your soul."

Steven Klein's ulcer began to pinch at his insides, and his face turned red with anger. But he held his tongue. His turn to speak would come soon enough.

Abe then reached into a shelf in the back of the lectern and pulled out a paper bag. And from the bag he removed a black velvet pouch with gold Hebrew letters embroidered on it, letters that spelled out the Kaddish, the mourner's prayer. And Abe opened up the pouch, and pulled out an old prayer shawl, the one with the word *Auschwitz* stitched into its side. And he draped the prayer shawl around his stooped shoulders, and began to pray.

"*Yisgadal v'yiskadash shmey rabo,*" he said. And the congregation repeated after him: "*Yisgadal v'yiskadash shmey rabo.*" "May his great name be magnified and sanctified," Abe said. And the congregation, again, repeated his words. And I looked at Norman-Meyer, and he looked at me. And we both looked at Eva, whose eyes were beginning to fill with tears.

"O merciful God," Abe said, beginning the prayer for the six million martyred. "On this solemn occasion of commemoration, we remember our brethren who were victims of the Nazi depravity. We see them in our mind's eye, marching before us, an endless procession of old and young; men, women, and children; scholars and sages; saints and housewives and tradesmen. We see them in the crematoriums of Buchenwald and Dachau, their torture-wracked bodies pulverized to ash. We see them in the mass-murder camps of Maidanek and Auschwitz, their last gasps of life choked by poison gas. They died proclaiming the unity of their God and the everlasting glory of His kingdom. If all the heavens were parchment, all the oceans ink, all the reeds pens, and all mankind writers, their praise could not be written down nor could the extent of their merit be told.

"O God," Abe continued, "may you remember meritoriously those who were slaughtered at the hands of the Nazis. May you avenge the spilled blood of your servants, as it is written in the Torah of Moses, the man of God: O nations, sing the praise of His people, for He will avenge the blood of his servants, and He will bring retribution upon His enemies, and He will appease His land and His people.

"And so, master of mercy, may you bind the souls of those who were slaughtered in the bond of eternal life. May the memory and piety of the righteous be eternal in your eyes. May peace come to them, and may they repose in peace upon their heavenly resting places. And let us say, Amen!"

"Amen," the congregation replied. And Abe Yellin clutched the black velvet pouch in his hand, retreated from the lectern, and returned to his seat.

The hall was completely still.

"Mr. Klein, I believe it's your turn," Rabbi Glickman said.

Steven Klein rose from his seat and approached the lectern. But before he got there, it started.

"You bastard!" shouted a man from the middle of the sanctuary. He jumped from his seat and rushed toward the stage. A Skokie cop had to restrain him. Another man yelled, "Klein, you're a traitor! You're scum!" General disorder ensued, and Klein stood back from the lectern to wait it out. His eye caught the glance of a neatly dressed old man who sat in the front row. The man smiled at Klein and gave him the finger.

After five minutes had passed, things had calmed down enough for Klein to begin.

"Ladies and gentlemen," he said, "I am not here to defend the views of Frank Collin or of the Nazi Party. I am here to . . ."

"Bullshit," someone yelled. The audience, whose anger seemed to be escalating, clapped its approval.

"I am here," Steven Klein said, "to defend just one thing, and that is the First Amendment. The First . . ."

"The First Amendment doesn't belong to Nazis!" screamed a woman. Again, shouts of approval and applause.

"The First Amendment, madam, belongs to everybody," Klein said, trying to contain his temper. "And that is the point of this whole controversy. Please, think about it for a moment. If you, the citizens of Skokie, allow your government to take the First Amendment away from Frank Collin, that very same government can sure as day take it away from you if they see fit."

Boos and hisses now rose from the sanctuary. "Stop being so arrogant!" someone yelled. Klein again stood back from the lectern. Rabbi Glickman went to the microphone. "Please, friends, we may disagree with our guest, but we should, in the name of fairness, let him speak."

"This is a war, Rabbi." It was Shmuel Ruderman speaking. Shmuel was a survivor of Dachau, and a member of the Korczak Unit. He stood up from his seat in the third row and pointed a finger at Steven Klein.

"You weren't there, Mr. Klein. You do not understand. We are a special breed of people, people who went through unbelievable things. History doesn't even know the things that happened to us. Your position, as a Jew, is beyond belief. It's all well and good to invoke the First Amendment and free speech. Those are fine things. But the purpose of writing the First Amendment was not for the Nazis, not for people who call for new ghettos and new concentration camps. I agree, a person should have a right to express an opposite opinion of the government, an opposite opinion of your own opinion. But it's impossible to think that the people who wrote the Constitution would say that a murderer has the right to come to your home and express his opinion and to say that we are going to murder a certain segment of people. I cannot believe that."

"Those who won our independence," Steven Klein replied, "believed that the freedom to think as you will and to speak as you think are means indispensable to the discovery and spread of political truth. Those are not my words," he said. "Those are the words of another Jew. Perhaps you've heard of him, sir. His name is Louis Brandeis, one of the greatest jurists ever to serve on the Supreme Court of these United States. And it was Brandeis, a Jew, who more than anyone else in this country's history stood for the First Amendment. For Brandeis, free speech was the secret of liberty. Brandeis said that the way to counter extreme ideas is through free and open public discussion, and not through government censorship or government ordinances. The fitting remedy for evil counsels is good ones, he said. I ask you, all of you here tonight, to consider that, to think about that."

A young woman rose from the side of the auditorium. "Maybe he's right," she said. "We shouldn't dignify Frank Collin by responding as we have, with all this fire and fury. We are a free people, and may I suggest that our best response to the Nazis would be to exercise the freedom to ignore them. They're just a handful of simpleminded morons out for publicity. They pose no threat. Let's not give them a power they don't have. Let them say what they will. Let them stand in front of our village hall and walk circles around themselves. We should choose simply not to show up. We should have the courage not to listen to them, not to pay them attention. Let them talk themselves dizzy all by themselves. Then they'll go home and leave us alone."

Martin Singer rose from the stage enraged. "You, young lady, are just as misguided as this so-called Jew from the civil liberties organization," he said. "You American-born Jews are so pious, so correct, but you know nothing. You may choose not to confront

Frank Collin, but we are survivors, and we will be there. Because our experience is superior to yours, and we cannot rely on your thinking. Because we know that normal thinking and understanding do not apply in this situation, which is irrational and insane. If the law does not protect us, we will protect ourselves. Never again will we sit on our hands and hope for the best! A nightmare is about to be reborn, and it must be stopped while it is small enough to stop!"

The young woman shriveled into her seat, buried by Martin Singer's words and by the explosion of cheers and applause that greeted them. The sanctuary filled with cries of "Never again! Never again!" Steven Klein left the lectern and tried to return to his chair as people began to fill the aisles and move toward the stage, whether to embrace Martin Singer and Abe Yellin or to assault Steven Klein nobody knew for sure. Somebody threw a water balloon at Klein, hitting him in the leg, and wetting his pants. The Skokie police moved in to contain the crowd, and a plainclothes detective ushered Klein off the stage and rushed him through a back corridor to the basement exit. Once outside, they were met by more plainclothesmen, who formed a cordon around Klein, and escorted him to his car. Two police cruisers followed Klein as he drove to the Skokie village limits. They abandoned him there, and Klein headed south, back to Chicago, and back to his wife. And that night he slept fitfully under the words of the First Amendment, amazed and troubled by the powers of emotion and of history and the unreasonableness and intolerance they can breed.

CHAPTER 5

The Cold War

There are some events in the life of a community that so sear the consciousness of its people and stick so tenaciously to their collective memory that years later, with hindsight and reflection, those events, like the scent of an old lover's perfume, capture—in a moment—the essence of a time, place, or era. In Skokie, during my lifetime, there were two such events. The Temple Shalom forum was one. Nothing so symbolized the frenzy and anger and fear associated with the threatened Nazi march and the long effort to stop it. But the second event, no less compelling, took place years earlier, in 1962. The holocaust at issue was nuclear, not Jewish. And for the first time in my young life, I realized that I could die.

The helicopter assault on Skokie, which came in the midst of the Cuban missile crisis, never really killed anyone, as far as I know. And it never drew the world's attention, like the Nazi controversy did. But the assault was extraordinary, nonetheless, confounding the generals, bewildering the troops, and fraying the nerves of more than a few citizens, who, to this day, remember where they were and what they were doing when the war birds first whooshed overhead.

Norman-Meyer and I were ten years old back then, prepubescent children of a twentieth-century suburban shtetl, and children, too, of the cold war. The war against communism shaped our lives as much as anything in those days. And I suppose, in a way, Chairman Khrushchev had as much to say about who we were, how we lived, and what we thought as Rabbi Glickman did, or Reb Rappoport, or any other community leader. Maybe even Grandpa Abe.

We all hated Khrushchev. Even us kids. We knew that he had the look and smell of a dangerous adversary: fat, bald, demented, greasy, cootielike. We knew that his rhetoric was scary, threatening us as he did with his "We shall bury you!" diatribes. And scarier still, we knew that Khrushchev was prone to crazy and bellicose behavior. After all, a man who would take his shoe off and bang it like a jackhammer at the United Nations was capable of anything.

At school, we reaffirmed in lessons what our national leaders had told us in speeches and what our parents had taught us at home: that communism was evil, that Marx and Lenin and Stalin and Khrushchev were pariahs of history, that Russians were different from us and weren't to be trusted, that the Kremlin was out to dominate the world. Mrs. Smith once asked us to write an essay titled "Who Are the Russians?" We responded with appropriate patriotic fervor. "The Russians are evil." That insight from me. "The Russians are bad, like Hitler, and they want to take away our freedom." That from Eva Singer. "The Russians are mean and they starve their children." That from Norman-Meyer Ashkenaz.

We even had a little song we sang back then about the USSR. Norman-Meyer was especially fond of the ditty, for it taunted and targeted somebody other than himself. He'd walk around the hallways of East Prairie Grammar and Junior High like a tubby little wandering minstrel, warbling the words with high-pitched abandon and encouraging one and all to join in the fun. The song went to the tune of "Whistle While You

Work" and exactly voiced our sentiments about the Soviet
leader:

> Whistle while you work,
> Khrushchev is a jerk,
> JFK will find a way to make him go berserk.

> Khrushchev picks his nose,
> That's the way it goes,
> Russians say that that's okay he'll wipe it on his clothes.

We were, in short, consumed by the Soviet threat. Arguably,
it rivaled Judaism as a presence in our lives. How could it be otherwise? We, the Jews of Skokie, were preoccupied with issues of
survival. Centuries of anti-Semitism and expulsions and ghettos
ensured that that was the case. So did the death camps, and the
death camp survivors who lived next door to us, or down the
street, or on the next block. Hitler was gone, yes. But in our cold
war world, the Russians were there, and they could do us in too.

In our book, the Soviets weren't much better than the Germans. Anti-Semitism in Russia had long, deep roots, and we
knew that firsthand. When my grandpa Abe was a boy, for instance, Lubeshov, his hometown, was under Russian, not Jewish, control. Abe had sharp memories of those times, and he'd
tell me of the cossacks who had ridden through his village, ran-
sacking the Jewish shops.

"Bobby, the fact is that anti-Semitism is ingrained in the
veins and minds of the Russian masses," Abe said. "I remember
when I was a child, some of the younger Jews wanted to organize a resistance group to fight the Russians. The elders of the
community wouldn't allow that, for fear of aggravating the situation. I remember my mother, in her simplistic way, criticizing

that attitude. She'd say to us, in Russian, *'Oni byut i plakat ne dayut,* We get beaten but we have no right to cry out.' "

Our obsession with the Russians might have been purely academic but for one indisputably troubling fact: Khrushchev had the bomb. And, thanks to *Sputnik,* we assumed he had the means to deliver it, with impeccable precision, through the windows and doors of our homes, stores, and synagogues. Oh, what a monstrous thing it was, we thought, that crazy Nikita had his pudgy little fingers on the nuclear button. And to make matters worse, there was the missile gap, and we were on the wrong side of it, at least so we were told. And on top of all that, enter Yuri Gagarin. His heroic exploits above us in outer space seemed disturbingly Big Brother-like. Yes, it's true that we had our own astronauts, and they were swell. But the Kremlin always seemed to come in first, and that left us feeling second-rate, scared, and terribly vulnerable.

So we adjusted our lives accordingly.

We lived, for one, under the proud and watchful gaze of the Forty-ninth Armored Anti-Aircraft Battery, skillfully commanded by Lt. Col. Edmund C. Campbell. The Forty-ninth Triple A, as it was called, consisted of four ninety-millimeter guns, situated at the corner of Grove and Kilbourn Streets, in the fashionable north-central part of Skokie. The guns faced northward, toward the polar cap, ready to shoot down anything the Russians might send our way.

Here's how the *Skokie News* described their mission, in an article headlined "49th AAA's Guns Sweep Sky for Skokie's Defense": "One of the ingredients of modern living is defense," the paper said. "Skokie is keeping pace with the demands of the times. The 49th AAA is here for one purpose—the defense against enemy aircraft of the northern sector of the Chicago area."

The paper stressed that "defense is a twenty-four-hour-a-day

job that knows no vacation." It said that Skokie's "ground de-
fenders are aware of the need for perpetual readiness and have
on the post at all times a minimum of forty-six men."

The paper reported that the Forty-ninth paid special attention to maintaining the mechanical fitness of its fighting equipment. "To assure perfect harmony of skilled gunmanship and
operational accuracy," the paper said, "Lt. Col. Campbell moves
his men and guns to Camp Haven, Wisconsin, every four months.
There the men and equipment go through exhaustive tests to ensure instantaneous readiness if an emergency should occur."

It was heady stuff, and the community embraced the Forty-
ninth Battery enthusiastically. They were *our* troops, and wherever the men of the Forty-ninth went, they were greeted with
warmth and affection. Nobody even cared that the soldiers
weren't Jewish, as long as they left our women alone.

The Temple Shalom sisterhood, for instance, contributed
cakes, flowers, shrubbery, and even a piano to the Forty-ninth's
base. "A mess hall shouldn't be messy," said Betty Rothstein, the
sisterhood's treasurer. "Let roses and sweet desserts bloom there,
and let the joy of music fill the air," she said.

At Rabbi Glickman's invitation, Lieutenant Colonel Campbell once addressed a post-Sabbath gathering in the temple's
main sanctuary. The colonel was a tall, bulky, narrow-eyed
man—a looming and intimidating presence. But he charmed the
crowd by removing his signature helmet and donning a yar-
mulke, the traditional Jewish skullcap. The colonel then read a
lecture titled "Communism: Our Mortal Enemy." Afterward, he
dined on chicken soup, brisket, and Vernor's ginger ale with
synagogue leaders. From that point on, a grateful Reb Rappoport, the itinerant Orthodox prophet who'd attended the
dinner, included the Forty-ninth on his daily rounds, bowing respectfully before the battery's four howitzers, and blessing the
guns with the prayer "Blessed art Thou, Lord our God, King of

the Universe, who keeps this arsenal strong, its aim true, and the dirty Communists at bay. *Tui! Tui! Tui!"*

As pleased as we were to have the Forty-ninth on our northern flank, the Soviet threat required additional diligence on the part of each and every one of us. For their part, Skokie officials surveyed the village for appropriate bomb shelter sites. They also ordered weekly air-raid drills. At 10:30 each Tuesday morning, sirens would scream their various songs all over the village—one long, mournful wail to warn of incoming nuclear missiles, and a series of cheerier beeps when all was clear. Sometimes at school, when the sirens went off, we'd head down the stairs to the East Prairie basement and huddle under long, laminated wooden cafeteria tables, covering our heads with our arms, and shutting our eyes to reality and the bright flash of light that would announce a nuclear blast.

School districts throughout the village also offered civil defense classes for our parents. "Education for Survival" is what they were called. Classes consisted of six two-hour sessions, and instructors covered, in the words of one course syllabus, "the basics of nuclear weapons and how to protect against them." Students also learned about "protective measures to be taken against conventional and biological warfare."

The press, always an integral part of any community, did its part to educate us about our enemies. The *Skokie Review*, one of several local newspapers, was particularly vocal in this regard. This article, for instance, appeared in August 1962:

In a speech delivered recently and reproduced here as a public service in America's widening battle against the menace of imperialistic communism, J. Edgar Hoover, director of the Federal Bureau of Investigation said: "It is an incontestable fact that our country, the symbol of the free world, is the ultimate, priceless goal of international communism. The leaders of international communism have vowed to achieve world domination. This cannot be until the Red flag is flown over the United States."

Hoover went on to say that the Communists planned "to conquer the United States, if not today, then tomorrow; if not tomorrow, then the next day, next month, next year." He warned that a Communist victory would reproduce the excesses of Hitler's Germany, realizing, in short order, the physical annihilation of whole classes of people. Lawyers, journalists, government officials, businessmen, and police officers would all perish, he said. "The list of purging is endless. No citizen would escape some form of suffering under a Communist regime."

Our parents did what they could to prepare for the worst. A few of the wealthier families in Skokie invested in fallout shelters. For a one-time fee of twenty-five hundred dollars, they purchased underground bunkers with concrete roofs, two feet thick, right there in their own backyards. One zealous citizen, Richard O'Keene, even concocted a plan to build a communal survival shelter, a sort of thermonuclear country club that would open its doors only to dues-paying members. The price tag was three hundred dollars. "Nonmembers will be kept out of club blast shelters by force if necessary," Mr. O'Keene said. He said his shelters would provide protection against nuclear missiles and "the mobs of underprivileged that will certainly scourge the area after an attack."

For those who couldn't afford such protection, more modest measures seemed appropriate. My mother, for instance, had the Temple Shalom sisterhood organize a "stock your basement shelves for survival" campaign. The ladies prepared a list of nonperishable kosher items that, in their estimation, would help

Jewish families ride out a nuclear attack. The list included canned beans, canned chicken soup, powdered milk, chocolate bars, dried prunes, kosher pickles and salamis, and, for the wintertime, preserved *schmaltz*, a chicken-fat concoction that was capable of sustaining Jewish life in much in the same way that whale blubber was known to preserve Eskimo culture. On the fourth Sunday of each month, the sisterhood women would fan out all over the village, knocking on doors and handing out survival packets to any family that wanted one.

To bolster our nation's defense, many of our parents also bought savings bonds, affordable, risk-free treasury instruments that offered modest rates of interest and a guarantee that the Pentagon would use the invested dollars "to protect the things America stands for and to make sure that you and your family will always enjoy the freedoms which a handful of brave Americans set their names to on July 4, 1776." Joseph Ashkenaz, Norman-Meyer's father, was particularly passionate about purchasing these so-called liberty bonds. He actually hoarded the things, like a crazed Red-hating hunter-gatherer, amassing in several years a small fortune in thousand-dollar certificates that were made out exclusively to "Joseph Ashkenaz with no right of survivorship." Joseph never told his wife, Fanya, about his wealth, and he kept the bonds in his separate bedroom, underneath a mattress, right next to his hunting rifle.

As for us kids, we too felt obliged to join the fight on behalf of liberty against communism. So we donated our teeth. It had little to do with dentistry and everything to do with nuclear weapons.

In the late fifties and early sixties, the Soviet Union and the United States conducted nuclear tests in the atmosphere, and they did so with increasing vigor. The blasts produced radioactive debris, which fell to the ground in the form of nuclear fallout. Our stuff fell on the Russians. And their stuff fell on us.

(And our stuff, we learned years later, fell on us, too.) And it layered our grasslands, and our cows ate that grass, and the radioactive junk entered our cows' milk. Later, when we drank that milk, the fallout entered us. It even tainted the breast milk of our milk-drinking mothers.

The milk-laden poisons went by different names: Carbon 14. Iodine 131. And strontium 90. It turned out that strontium 90 accumulates in bones, bone marrow, and teeth. So in 1958, Dr. Herman M. Kalckar of the Harvard University Medical School suggested that kids could help the cause of freedom by donating their baby teeth to science, so that science could measure just how successful the Russians had been in poisoning our population. (Or, as we learned years later, just how successful we'd been in poisoning ourselves.)

The study was organized by the Washington University School of Dentistry in St. Louis, Missouri. So it was to that great midwestern city that we dispatched our little choppers. By 1962, the peak year for aboveground nuclear blasts, Mrs. Joseph Logan, director of the Baby Tooth Survey, reported collecting baby teeth at a rate of seven hundred a week.

Ben Zuboff was one of Skokie's most prominent dentists, and his wife, Ida, took upon her shoulders the task of coordinating the village baby-teeth collection drive. Up until then, Ida was not particularly well regarded in the community, largely because she was her husband's dental hygienist. From our point of view, God had pretty much placed Ida Zuboff on earth to inflict pain on adults and kids alike by unartfully scouring our teeth and gums for germ-laden tartar. We called her Mrs. Blood.

But the skill and grace with which Ida Zuboff managed the baby-teeth collection drive rehabilitated her reputation. She promoted the effort with the slogan "Take a Bite Out of Communism," and gave away free Tootsie Rolls to every child who deposited a tooth at her husband's office. When word spread that she was dealing in twelve-packs of Tootsie Roll pops and dispensing, additionally, those big, long, meaty, segmented Tootsie Roll bars (not the tiny, individually wrapped nuggets), the children of Skokie responded as you might have expected: scores of six and seven year olds with pothole smiles queued up to cash in, along with their older brothers and sisters, whose molars had finally given out. Norman-Meyer, whose affection for Tootsie Rolls wouldn't surprise you, even asked Fanya, his mother, if she might allow Dr. Zuboff to extract a few extra teeth for a few extra bites of that poisonous Tootsie Roll apple. Fanya said no, and her husband threatened to knock out Norman-Meyer's bicuspids if he disobeyed.

The results of the tooth survey disquieted our village. Strontium 90 was indeed in our bodies, and nobody knew whether enough had accumulated to cause cancer. The government's Federal Radiation Council, however, reported that strontium 90 ingestion in the Midwest was within the "safe" range.

Nothing, though—not the Baby Tooth Survey, not the savings bond purchases, not the fallout shelters or the air-raid drills or the men of the Forty-ninth Triple A, and certainly not the media—prepared Skokie for the Cuban missile crisis and all that accompanied it. I suppose Mannie Goodstein and the rest of the Oakton Street merchants deserved some credit for their readiness and foresight, not to mention their dramatic sense of timing, because their promotional scheme unfolded in the very midst of those anxious October days. If attention is what they sought, then they emerged from the crisis full-fledged, banner-headlined public figures, and their businesses, I suppose, may have profited in the end. But in the short run, nobody in Skokie, with the exception of the more stouthearted village children, could honestly say they had gained from the mess.

That Khrushchev chose Cuba to challenge America wasn't all that surprising. He and his Latin puppet, Fidel Castro, were, after all, perfectly matched: Nikita, the domineering and rotund Hardy, to Fidel's emotionally manic and frail Laurel. The two Communist leaders seemed so inseparable that once, in school, at a mock United Nations, Norman-Meyer and I decided to play the duo. We were good friends, and so were Nikita and Fidel, so the matchup seemed natural.

Norman-Meyer, of course, played the role of Khrushchev. He pinned a red star made out of construction paper onto his chest and roamed around our make-believe General Assembly Hall boinking the delegates of lesser-developed nations with his big old belly, literally pushing them out of the way with well-timed pelvic thrusts that had the effect of sending his stomach full force into and through the body of anyone daring to get in its way. And I, as Fidel, followed in Norman-Meyer's wake, clutching one of my uncle Ted's cigars and wearing my dad's old army cap and a taped-on, black crepe-paper beard. "Viva Nikita! Viva Nikita!" I shouted, as Norman-Meyer continued the business of burying nations and dominating the world.

I really didn't do Fidel justice, however, for I was a bit restrained in my portrayal. Castro, in fact, struck us in real life as a complete psychopath, a hot-tempered ranter prone to fiery-eyed, arm-waving tirades against his imperialist neighbor to the north. Martin Singer used to say that Castro reminded him of Hitler: both Castro and Hitler had a dictator's propensity to shout themselves hoarse while delivering speeches, and both had aberrant facial hair.

So did Mannie Goodstein, age thirty-eight, who wore a chin beard without a mustache and fashioned himself the Skokie doyen of the beat generation. Mannie owned the Oakton Bakery, whose ovens produced the bagels and challah and rye bread and wedding cakes that fueled Jewish life in our village. He also hosted occasional poetry readings at the shop, whose gray plaster walls were brightened with tacked-on berets of various colors and sizes and with *Life* magazine photographs of Jack Kerouac and Allen Ginsburg. Mannie's salons afforded the dozen or so aging beatniks in town a chance to sip coffee, socialize, and read aloud their latest rhymes against propriety and injustice. Mannie once invited my grandpa Abe to a poetry reading; so great was Abe's artistic stature that even the beatniks admired him. My grandfather was eager to fit in, so he showed up in a tie and a sleeveless cardigan and read to the group a protest poem he'd written especially for the occasion:

> Master of the Universe, Creator of heaven and earth,
> In your hands are death and birth;
> You had created man and beast,
> They need each other—to say the least.
>
> You gave us the sun, so warm and bright,
> The moon, to illuminate the darkness at night,
> Countless twinkling little stars
> Accompanying giant Jupiter and Mars.
> Clouds to supply us with spring showers,
> They turn dry thorns into blooming flowers.
>
> The world is beautiful—nothing is wrong:
> Only the inhabitants can't get along.

For all of Mannie's devotion to the bohemian lifestyle, he was a pragmatist at heart, and he never let the beat get in the way of earning a buck. He founded the Oakton Street Merchants Association in 1959 in order "to further promote fellowship and commerce among Skokie's Jewish entrepreneurial pioneers." The organization had nineteen members, including the owners of Cohen's Hardware, Dosik's Dry Cleaners, Irving's Chevrolet, Sol's Five and Dime, and Moshe Kapinsky's Discount

Shoe Store. The group was diverse in age and outlook, and Kapinsky hated Cohen because Cohen's son Ira had recently impregnated Kapinsky's daughter Deborah. But the men all shared a taste for self-promotion, for through self-promotion came business, and business meant money.

The helicopter scheme was Mannie's idea. It came to him one Sunday afternoon in October while he and his son Mannie Jr. were playing Ping-Pong in the rec room of their two-story home. Junior was ten years old and a precocious little boy, and he loved to slam the Ping-Pong ball as hard as he could. With the score five-zip in Junior's favor, the little guy let loose with a forehand return that sent the white plastic ball at cometlike speed straight into Mannie's noggin. It was a eureka moment for the Oakton Street baker, and he convened a meeting of the merchants association the next day to sell his idea.

"Gentlemen, here's what I think we should do," Mannie said. "We get ten thousand Ping-Pong balls and fill them with all kinds of goodies to lure in the customers. Discount coupons, mostly. But cash, too. Maybe even a couple hundred-dollar bills. And we hire some helicopters to fly over Skokie and drop the balls like manna from heaven all over town. And the people will chase those things like a bunch of horny old rabbis let loose in the ladies' side of a Russian steam bath. And they'll take their booty and run on home and get into their cars and drive on down to our venerable places of business, and they'll spend all kinds of money they'd never planned to, all from the rush and excitement of those Ping-Pong balls falling down from the sky. Whaddya think?"

The merchants approved Mannie's proposal immediately and without dissent. Arrangements were made, Ping-Pong balls ordered and stuffed, helicopters and helicopter pilots leased, and the press notified. The date selected for the Ping-Pong-ball drop was Thursday, October 25, ten days thence.

Then came the Cuban missile crisis. On Monday, October 22—three days before the Ping-Pong-ball promotion—at 7:00 P.M. eastern time, President John F. Kennedy went on TV and told the people of Skokie and the rest of the country of the mischief Khrushchev and Castro had been up to.

"Good evening, my fellow citizens," Kennedy said. "This government, as promised, has maintained the closest surveillance of the Soviet military buildup on the island of Cuba. Within the past week, unmistakable evidence has established the fact that a series of offensive missile sites is now in preparation on that imprisoned island. The purpose of these bases can be none other than to provide a nuclear strike capability against the Western Hemisphere.

"The characteristics of these new missile sites indicate two distinct types of installations," Kennedy said. "Several of them include medium-range ballistic missiles, capable of carrying a nuclear warhead for a distance of more than one thousand nautical miles. Each of these missiles, in short, is capable of striking Washington, D.C., the Panama Canal, Cape Canaveral, Mexico City, or any other city in the southeastern part of the United States. . . .

"Additional sites not yet completed appear to be designed for intermediate-range ballistic missiles—capable of traveling more than twice that far—and thus capable of striking most of the major cities in the Western Hemisphere."

Kennedy said Khrushchev's decision to base nuclear missiles in Cuba was a deliberate provocation, one that America would challenge. He ordered the United States Navy to blockade Cuba and to intercept any additional offensive military equipment en route to the island. He warned that any nuclear missile launched from Cuba against any nation in the Western Hemisphere would be regarded as an attack on the United States "requiring a full retaliatory response upon the Soviet Union."

"I call upon Chairman Khrushchev to halt and eliminate a reckless and provocative threat to world peace and to stable relations between our two nations," Kennedy said. "We have no wish to war with the Soviet Union, for we are a peaceful people who desire to live in peace with all other peoples. . . . Our goal is not the victory of might, but the vindication of right. . . . God willing, that goal will be achieved."

The speech was powerful and sobering. I remember watching it with Norman-Meyer, who'd come over for dinner that evening. We sat on the bed in my room in front of a little Sears black-and-white, and we remained silent as the president spoke. Neither of us understood much about politics or diplomacy or ballistic missiles. But we knew that Kennedy was confronting the Russians, and we knew that JFK wouldn't back down. The president spoke of war and of nuclear retaliation. He actually used those words. And we were scared, for we knew that the Russians were strong, and that their missiles might actually fly. And we knew that Nikita would aim them at us, for we lived by Chicago, and Chicago would certainly be targeted.

"I'm afraid, Bobby," Norman-Meyer said.

"So am I," I replied.

"Do you think we'll die?" he asked.

"I don't know," I said. "I think we will."

And we both sat there, imagining the nuclear holocaust that m' h soon destroy us. What would it feel like? we wondered. Would it hurt to die that way? And Norman-Meyer began to shake. And I put my arm around him, and lay my head against his shoulder. And we both closed our eyes, hoping, somehow, that the self-imposed darkness would shield us from harm.

Skokie immediately went on a virtual-war footing. At least it seemed that way. At school, we retreated to the basement cafeteria shelter once a day. In the synagogues there were special prayer vigils, imploring God to protect us, and to give our president the strength and courage to do what needed to be done. The local press carried articles about "The Bomb," and what it might do to our community if it hit.

"Out to about four miles from 'ground zero' would be an area of virtually complete devastation with all buildings destroyed and probably complete loss of life," the *Skokie Review* said. "Severe blast damage would extend to about six miles from ground zero and blast damage in varying degrees to ten miles. Numerous fires would quickly develop at various locations out to about twelve miles from ground zero." The paper printed an aerial photograph of Skokie with this caption: "Using Weller's Motel at Touhy, Caldwell and Gross Point Rd. as ground zero, a ten-megaton ground burst would dig a crater and a rupture zone, and every house, factory, school, etc., in this entire picture would be totally destroyed."

Considering all that was going on, who could blame the editors of that and other newspapers for burying Mannie Goodstein's notice about the Oakton Street merchants' impending promotional event? On Tuesday, October 23, the *Skokie News* had only this small item on page 12, beneath the fold, with a headline that read, "It's Raining, It's Pouring Ping-Pong Balls": "Ping-Pong balls will rain down on Skokie, Thursday, October 25, at 10 A.M." the paper said. "Inside each of the 10,000 balls will be merchandise certificates for special values in Oakton Street stores. Some of the balls will have hundred-dollar bills inside them. Stores will remain open Friday and Saturday nights so everyone finding balls may take advantage of the bargains. Helicopters will be used to drop the Ping-Pong balls over residential Skokie neighborhoods."

I don't think anyone ever read that article. Certainly not Mrs. Millie Kupferman, or she wouldn't have hyperventilated so badly when she looked out her living room window that Thursday morning and saw three choppers hovering aloft like a troika of howling dragonflies ready to strike. And Capt. Sam Schmidt of the Skokie Police Department, who took Mrs. Kupferman's call, never saw the notice, for when Millie screamed, "The Russians are attacking! They're sending helicopters over Skokie and they're bombing my house!" Captain Schmidt, a Korean War vet and a VFW leader, responded with credulity, ordering two squad cars over to Mrs. Kupferman's neighborhood stat. And when Officers Polansky and Meyer—who never, ever read the newspaper—first saw the war birds overhead, they figured Millie Kupferman had gotten it right, and they radioed their boss that the village was indeed under assault and that "the Russkies or someone" was shooting "white bullets and missiles all over the friggin' place!" And when Captain Schmidt sounded the general alarm and urgently telephoned Lt. Col. Edmund C. Campbell of the Skokie Forty-ninth Armored Anti-Aircraft Battery, Col. Campbell hadn't read the article, and he couldn't, because he and the valiant soldiers of the Forty-ninth had abandoned their posts five days earlier for field maneuvers in Camp Haven, Wisconsin. Thus Skokie lost any and all hope of saving itself by shooting the helicopters down.

The panic that swallowed our village increased exponentially as the hailstorm of Ping-Pong balls shrouded our streets, homes, and yards, and left us terrified and confused. Reb Rappoport, poor old Reb Rappoport, was caught dead to rights by the attacking copters. He was, as usual, walking the streets on his appointed rounds at ten that morning, and as the din of rotor blades and pellets of white plastic spheroids came upon him, he froze: a bearded, black-garbed Orthodox mannequin, legs all noodlelike, arms stretched skyward, Ping-Pong balls bouncing *bop-bip-bop* off the broad, round brim of his *streyml*, or Orthodox cap. "Roosh-ee-ahns!" he screamed, helpless before the onslaught. "Roosh-ee-ahns!" he howled. "Oy, oy, oy!" he cried. "Oy, oy, oy!"

Automobiles lurched and screeched as anxious drivers tried to make sense of it all. A six-car pileup blocked the intersection of Howard and Crawford, at the edge of our neighborhood. On our block, people began pouring from their houses, the horrible clatter of Ping-Pong balls pounding mercilessly on their roofs overwhelming them with fear. Our mothers were home alone that day—most of their husbands were working—and that fact made them all the more skittish. Clusters of frazzled ladies—Cohens and Zimmers and Liechtensteins, Schwabs and Levys and Milsteins—ran around their yards and each other in various states of undress and bewilderment, dodging the bullets as best they could, and grasping each other for comfort.

"Fallout!" Sofie Milstein screamed. "Radioactive fallout! We're going to die! We're going to die!"

The air-raid sirens had started to howl when Miriam, my mother, found Beatrice Singer sitting alone on her front porch, praying. The two women could barely hear each other above the sound of the copters. So they huddled together, muttering the *shema*, the Jewish invocation of God Almighty, and they shivered in chilled anticipation of the nuclear blast they believed imminent. Miriam wondered how her parents, Abe and Emma, were faring, and she imagined, correctly, that the two were lying in bed, in loving embrace, waiting for God to do his will.

Joseph Ashkenaz, Norman-Meyer's father, happened to be home that morning when the trio of spiral-winged aircraft roared overhead. So was his wife, Fanya. She reacted calmly to the attack, sitting quietly in her living room chair, relieved, somehow, that the end was near. Joseph, however, lost it. His mop of red hair burned in anger at the thought of anyone, let alone the Soviets, assaulting his home and the interest-bearing hidden treasure that lay there. Joseph took a swill of vodka—not his first that morning—and ran into his bedroom to grab his rifle. He rushed outside, slipping on some Ping-Pong balls that covered his sidewalk like fresh fallen snow.

"You fucking bastards!" Joseph shouted, picking himself up off the pavement. He aimed his rifle toward the skies, and he fired off six rounds in amazingly quick succession as the helicopters moved away. One of the shots clipped the front nose of the lead aircraft, rendering the pilot scared but the craft still airworthy. The rest of the bullets missed their mark.

Ernie O'Malley, skipper of the injured flying machine, looked back and saw a red-haired maniac waving a .22 this way and that. He radioed for help, and later, after the village came to its senses, Joseph Ashkenaz was arrested for assault with a deadly weapon.

Norman-Meyer and I were at school when the helicopters flew overhead. It was recess time, and scores of kids were outside, playing tag, swinging on swings, and running around wondering whether Khrushchev and Castro would let us live or die. Then the whoosh of the aircraft hit us, followed by waves of Ping-Pong balls. At first, we all started to scream. We were genuinely scared. But Ping-Pong balls aren't multiple warheads, and as curiosity got the best of us, we picked up those little plastic orbs, cracked them open, and discovered the prizes that rested within. When little Hermie Meinsdorf shouted, "Hey, I got a hundred bucks here!" we realized that Armageddon was not yet upon us, and, kids being kids, we began to have fun. We frolicked after those Ping-Pong balls like a bunch of jackrabbits, stuffing as many as we could in our hands and pockets. Norman-Meyer displayed unexpected and admirable vigor in his pursuit, finding a fleetness of foot that nobody had guessed he had. By the time it was over, we all were rich with valuable discount coupons for ice cream and comic books and hardware trinkets and the like, and the sheer frenzy of the chase was cathartic, and it eased the tension, if only briefly, of the crisis our country was still in the midst of.

We kids were probably the only residents of Skokie who appreciated Mannie Goodstein's harebrained helicopter scheme. When it was all over, when the helicopters left and the village returned to normal, the Oakton Street Merchants Association ousted Mannie as their leader, officially saying the reason had something to do with his health. But the real cause was the swell of negative publicity and public anger that followed the helicopter assault, publicity and anger that turned into a consumer boycott of Oakton Street stores. It was only after a public show of remorse by the association's members—and a pledge to reduce prices by 20 percent—that patrons again returned to their shops.

At the end of the day, the toll on our village from the affair was mostly emotional. It scared the bejesus out of the community, but little more. The mayor, however, did say in his "Special Report" on the matter that two people had been hospitalized with chest pains, thirty-five cars involved in minor fender benders, and eight thousand unbudgeted dollars spent in cleaning up Ping-Pong-ball droppings.

We were all grateful that nothing more serious had happened. And on Sunday, October 28, when Chairman Khrushchev announced he'd ordered the Cuban missiles dismantled and crated for return back home, we thanked God that our president had saved the day, and that America, and the Jews of Skokie, would not see another holocaust.

And a few weeks later, on Thanksgiving Day, my grandpa Abe gathered his clan around the dinner table, raised a cup of Manischewitz Concord grape, and pronounced this prayer:

Let us all thank God for our blessed land,
For our system of government that is grand;
For our bountiful resources and plentiful food,
For our beauty, and energy, and upbeat mood.

If it were taken to a test,
Our country would prove to be the best.
Thank God for our freedom in tranquillity and peace,
It sure beats communism, to say the least.

Amen.

CHAPTER 6

Gentiles

W hen God created Heaven and Earth, and from the rib of Adam woman he did make, surely no sweeter and lovelier creature emerged than Suzie Louise Anderson, my first love. When we met, I was seven and so was she, and our romance lasted two long years, until her parents moved to a farm in Wisconsin, and I was left behind in Skokie, bereft and heartbroken, determined never to marry, for never again would so fine a woman rattle my soul as Suzie Louise.

Suzie lived in a house on the other side of the alley from us, in a world on the other side of God. She was a Christian, one of the few non-Jews on our block. Fruit of the poisonous tree, so to speak, because a Jewish boy and a non-Jewish girl—a shiksa, in common parlance—were never to mingle or mate. That was the law, and all understood it. But we were young and the chance of tainted offspring negligible. So even my grandpa abided our union, however begrudgingly.

"She's a cute little goy," Abe said. Beyond that, though, he'd have nothing to do with her.

Truth be told, Suzie's belief in the Holy Trinity only enhanced her appeal to me. Her faith made her new and exciting and strange and exotic, totally unlike any other girl I'd ever met. She had blue eyes, the first blue eyes I'd known. And blonde hair, curly blonde hair that meandered and flowed like a river in paradise down to the back of her knees.

And her parents were different from mine. They ate donuts for breakfast, sweet, sugar-glazed yeast donuts, and I ate them too when I stayed overnight. And they buttered their bologna sandwiches. And they let me help decorate their Christmas tree, and even concocted a tinfoil Star of David ornament with my name on it. And most curiously and wonderfully of all, they came from a family of farmers, and they owned a horse and a goat and some chickens that they kept right there in their own backyard in Skokie. The horse's name was Buster, and I got to ride him up and down the alley between our houses until Norman-Meyer's father stepped on some horse manure one day while taking out the garbage. Joseph Ashkenaz complained to the police—"We don't need any goddamn gentile horse crap around here," he said—and the police, invoking a seventy-year-old ordinance prohibiting livestock from running at large within village limits, made the Andersons move their menagerie out to the country.

Suzie and I were a private couple and jealously guarded our time together. We did so because we were different, and our differences made us special. We did so because we were special, and wanted to live in our own special world. So we kept to ourselves, and wouldn't let Norman-Meyer or Eva Singer or any of the other kids on the block join in our games. We'd play jacks on the front porch of her house, and jump rope in the driveway and go round the world on rainy days in her living room with our yo-yos. We'd walk to school together, trading notes on the latest second- or third-grade gossip: how Billy Burmeister puked in the classroom; how Mrs. Krone made Sharon Brickman cry; how Norman-Meyer, good old Norman-Meyer, spilled a carton of chocolate milk over Sylvia Shamberg's head by mistake as he tried to shimmy himself, milk-laden lunch tray aloft in one hand, through a crowded basement cafeteria; and how Sylvia Shamberg subsequently retaliated by pouring her creamed corn down the front of Norman-Meyer's pants.

We'd play at Suzie's house mostly, for that's where Buster lived, and as I fed him carrots or squares of sugar, Suzie would tell me about summers on her family's farm, about fields of corn and a scarecrow named Oscar and a milk cow named Hazel and ice cream they'd make from scratch from the milk Hazel gave them. And once, I actually got to visit that farm and taste that ice cream. Suzie's parents invited me up, and my folks agreed. So we all rose early one Indian-summer Saturday morning in October, and I and Suzie and her parents and Buster drove five hours in a Chevy station wagon with a horse trailer hitched behind it to central Wisconsin and the Anderson family farm.

Suzie's uncle Tommy and aunt Becky ran the place, and they treated me most kindly, rube that I was. I got to squeeze Hazel's udder and ride Buster bareback and go canoeing in a real creek that ran through the property. I met my first pig on that farm— a tiny pet oinker named Piglet who ran all over the place and squealed with confidence and bravado and rightly so, for Uncle Tommy had trained the little guy to scurry down to the main road each day to retrieve, in his snout, the morning paper. The thing was so smart and so cute that I had to question why we Jews despised pigs so.

And for Saturday-night dinner we had food so curious and tasty that to this day I can still recall the menu: collard greens and panfried trout with corn bread and Mrs. Anderson's home-made sweet tomato chutney on the side. The trout was the coolest surprise, freshly caught that day and sitting there whole on my plate, smiling a little fishy smile at me, eyes staring side-ways the way fish eyes do, checking out the company gathered there to feast.

"I never had fish this way before," I said.

"Well, what do you all eat?" Uncle Tommy asked.

"Lox and gefilte mostly," I said.

"Well, Bobby," Uncle Tommy said, grinning, "I'da caught one of those for you if I coulda, but they don't swim up here in these parts."

And the next morning, before coming home, the Andersons asked me if I would like to go with them to church. And I immediately said yes, because I'd never been to church before, and it would be interesting to tell Grandpa Abe about the experience, theologian that he was. And what transpired there in that countryside chapel was surely quite interesting, the singing and kneeling and tapers and holy water and all, and especially neat was the thing at the end, with the wine and the wafers, which I insisted on tasting in the name of good fellowship and ecumenicalism. And the food went down smoothly, until later, when Suzie told me I'd more or less eaten the blood and flesh of the Lord Almighty, at which point I did get a bit queasy with indigestion.

But all told it was a most glorious weekend. And I returned to my village ever more entranced with Suzie Louise Anderson. And the Christian way of life she lived seemed ever more interesting and far less remote than it had before. Until one day some weeks later, in early December, when Suzie approached me during school recess, and asked me point-blank, with anguish-filled eyes and soft-spoken words: "Bobby, why did you kill Jesus Christ?"

The controversy over the abduction and presumed death of Jesus was reported in full in the morning edition of that day's local newspaper, the *Skokie Life*. I read it upon returning home from school. I immediately understood why Suzie had been so distraught. The front-page headline declared: "Jesus Snatched. Feared Dead. Crisis Looms." Here's what the article said:

The lifelike figure of the baby Jesus was stolen from the manger at the Christmas Nativity Scene on the Village Hall lawn, police said today.

The sixteen-inch, three-pound plaster likeness of the infant Christ was reported missing early this morning by Frankie Conroy, a Village Hall custodian. "I arrived for work as usual at five this morning and Jesus was gone," Conroy said. "I said to myself, somebody went and stole the Lord, so I called up the police as fast as I could."

A Skokie police spokesman, Sgt. Albert Warner, said no trace of Jesus had been found, and no ransom note left at the scene of the crime. He added that authorities fear for the worst.

The abduction of Christ comes amid a continuing controversy over the efficacy of the Skokie village board's decision last week to sponsor the Christmas Nativity display, or creche, on village property. The move triggered a loud outcry from Skokie's large Jewish community, which says that the village should stay out of the business of promoting religion.

"This is a community of Jews and Christians, and our government should not seem to be favoring one group over the other," said Rabbi Sidney Glickman of Temple Shalom. "In our system, church and state should remain separate, so the Nativity Scene should come down," he said.

Rabbi Glickman said he "regretted" the theft of the baby Jesus, and assured members of the Christian community that the overwhelming majority of Skokie's Jews do not condone illegal activities as a means to resolve the creche crisis.

Betty Thorpe, chairman of the creche organizing committee, angrily condemned the person or persons responsible for the crime. Asked if she thought a Jew had stolen Christ, Thorpe said: "I don't know. It wouldn't surprise me if that were the case."

A haggard Mayor Myron Greisdorf urged the community

to stay calm in the face of the latest developments. "I know that this creche affair has increased tensions between some factions in our town," he said. "We are all God-loving citizens, even if we worship different gods, and we ought to be able to settle this thing peaceably."

The Village Trustees issued a statement "abhorring any unlawful threat aimed at stirring up internal strife within the community."

The creche includes figures of Mary and Joseph, the three wise men, three sheep, and, until yesterday, the baby Jesus. None of the other figures were harmed as a result of the incident.

So Jesus was gone, whereabouts unknown, and for poor little Suzie Louise Anderson, the Savior appeared to be dead, for his manger lay brutally stripped, cold and bare, on the green at Village Hall. And, as her question to me at school recess suggested, the blame for such an affront lay squarely at my feet, and at the feet of every other Jew in Skokie, for we had opposed the nativity scene, and who but us would have gained from an act of deicide, however misguided?

When I saw Suzie the next morning, she was a little bit distant, the way nine-year-old girls get when they're angry at the men in their lives. She barely spoke on the way to school, and she bit her lower lip a lot. And those blue eyes of hers avoided all contact with mine, preferring instead the safety of the sidewalk or street.

"I'm really sorry about what happened with Jesus," I said finally, guessing the cause of her mood.

She stopped walking and turned to me, her eyes now directly fixed on mine. "Some of my parents' church friends came over to visit last night," she said.

"Yeah," I said.

"Jesus was all they could talk about."

"What did they say?" I asked.

She sighed, and bit her lip again. "They all said that the Jews did it, that the Jews took baby Jesus away from us, and probably murdered him."

I looked at her, not quite knowing how to respond. I was feeling guilty.

"Mr. O'Rourke was there," she continued. "You know him? His son Dennis is that big high school football star?"

"Yeah, he scored three touchdowns last week, one on a seventy-yard pass reception," I said, trying to brighten the tone of our conversation. "I betcha Dennis will play in the pros someday, don't you think? My dad says he'd fit in really well with the Bears 'cause they'll need a good receiver once Johnny Morris retires."

"Mr. O'Rourke was really angry," Suzie said.

"Even after Dennis scored three touchdowns?" I asked.

"Yes," she said curtly.

Suzie then told me what Mr. O'Rourke had said: that he and his family had lived in Skokie for twenty-five years; that they'd moved here long before most of the Jews; that now, in his view, the Jews just keep coming and coming; that they're trying to take over, and they're trying to push the Christians around. Suzie said Mr. O'Rourke spoke of Jewish successes in buying up Skokie businesses and electing a Jewish mayor, none of which, he said, made the Jews happy. And he said some of the village's Jewish residents even complained about prayers in the public schools.

"Mr. O'Rourke says the Jews have gone too far, by attacking the manger at Village Hall," Suzie said. "And he says Jews are Christ killers. And he said some other mean things, too."

She paused for a moment, trying, I think, to decide whether to tell me what those other things were.

"Anyway," she said, "a lot of the people at my house last night agreed with Mr. O'Rourke, although my parents told him to calm down. And I was upset with what he was saying, so I walked right up to him and said: 'No sir, Mr. O'Rourke. My boyfriend, Bobby, is a Jewish person, and he's not at all like what you say. He's got nothing against Jesus, and I know he doesn't object to Christmas, and he even went to church with us once. And his parents are really nice, too. They're not mean people, like you say.' And Mr. O'Rourke just looked at me and said I was too young to know what I was talking about, and that maybe I should go to bed. At which point my daddy asked him to leave. And later on, after everyone had gone and my daddy came to kiss me goodnight, I said to him, 'Daddy, why was Mr. O'Rourke so mean about the Jews?' And he said that there are some people who are just like that, and to pay them no mind. And I asked my daddy whether Mr. O'Rourke was right, that the Jews had taken Jesus away from us. And my daddy said it could be that a Jewish person stole the Christ child, and that was an awful thing to do. And he said he thought it was wrong for the Jews to oppose the nativity scene, too. But he said he hoped things would work out okay in the end."

Suzie drew silent again and turned away from me. I reached for her hand, and she let me hold it, interlocking her pinky with mine.

"You didn't steal Jesus, did you, Bobby?" she asked. "I mean, you didn't have anything to do with it, right, even though you're Jewish?"

"No, of course not," I said.

"And the nativity scene, do you have anything against that?"

"Nope," I said. I hadn't even known that the thing was in

Skokie until just the day before, and I couldn't see how its being there affected my life one way or the other, other than the negative way it was affecting me right now, with Suzie being so upset over the Jesus kidnapping. And I figured that until this thing was fixed to her liking, Suzie would continue to be one unhappy and discouraged young lady, which, considering my feelings about her, would make me one unhappy and discouraged young man. So I resolved right then and there to do something about it.

"Don't worry, Suzie Louise," I said. "Things will turn out okay. You'll see."

And we made our way to school. And I sought the counsel of my friend Norman-Meyer, whose help I needed as I prepared to go out in search of Jesus Christ.

I located Norman-Meyer at lunchtime, huddled over a plate of hot dogs, french fries, potato chips, and Twinkies.

"I need to find Jesus," I said.

"Huh?" he replied.

"I need to find Jesus. He's vanished, kidnapped, maybe dead, and Suzie's upset. So I need to find him."

Norman-Meyer bit into a Twinkie. "How do you plan to do that?" he asked.

"A posse," I said. "And I need your help."

He finished the cream-filled pastry and wiped his mouth with his sleeve. "Jeez, Bobby, I don't know," he said.

"Look," I said, "you're going to help me because you're my friend and the Christian savior is missing and you have no choice in the matter, because if you don't help me and there's anything to this Christian stuff, who knows, maybe you'll go to hell. So we've got to find Jesus, okay?"

He could see I meant business. "Okay," he said. "But don't tell my father. So what do we need to do?"

"First off," I said, "I need information. You're smarter than anyone else around here. So tell me what you know."

"What I know about what?" he asked.

"Jesus, Norman-Meyer, what you know about Jesus," I said.

Norman-Meyer crinkled his brow, adjusted his glasses, closed his eyes, and thought for a moment. "I think he was Jewish," he said.

"Jesus was Jewish?" I asked.

"Yep. He was Jewish. Pretty neat, huh?"

Now I was stumped. Jesus was Jewish. Christians love Jesus. Jews don't love Jesus. But Jesus was Jewish. It was confusing, and I wanted to know more about this man whom Suzie worshiped. Why did he move her so? Why would someone—a Jew, no less—try to remove him? How could I find him? But the fact of the matter was that it was hard for a Jewish kid to divine the meaning of Christ when Christ, for most Jews, stood squarely aloof, or aloft, as it were, as the resurrected son of an alien, offensive God.

I came from a culture that reacted viscerally to the notion of Christ, for Christ, in the view of our fathers, was pretty much solely responsible for the sufferings of our people. The logic was specious, but appealing: without Christ, there would have been no Christians; Christians, from the Crusades through the Inquisition to the pogroms of our grandparents, persecuted Jews; Christ and Christianity, therefore, were to blame for centuries of anti-Semitism. To our elders, then, it was straightforward and simple: all Christians were goyim—the pejorative label for non-Jews—and they were, to our minds, all pretty much alike. And we, pretty much, kept away from them, and to ourselves.

There was, of course, no de jure segregation in Skokie, as in the South. Nor was the separation clearly de facto, for the Jews and Christians of our village did interact: in the marketplace, in public arenas, and at schools. The Christians, in fact, were all over the place, and their houses of worship stood everywhere our synagogues weren't, defining with steeples and stained-glass windows the neighborhoods we didn't live in. There were Catholic churches, and churches for Lutherans and Episcopalians and Presbyterians and Methodists and even a church for Christian Scientists. This dizzying cacophony of Jesus worship was just plain bewildering, and reinforced a sense that Christians were different from us.

The issue arose in a graphic and innocent way at school one day, when we'd just begun gym class and had to endure, for the first time in our young lives, the humbling locker room trauma of showering naked before our peers. It was an experience that none of us relished, for nudity, we believed, was a private thing, best left in the home. Modesty, in fact, was a matter of Jewish tradition. "There's nothing more disgraceful or detestable for a man than to appear naked in public." That's what the Talmud, the collection of Jewish laws, said. But the Talmud had no jurisdiction in Skokie's public schools, so naked we became, however reluctantly, in the East Prairie boys' gymnasium locker room.

We all looked, of course. At each other's bodies. At each other's body parts. And at Johnny Murphy's penis, which was uncircumcised. Johnny had a lot of explaining to do when that secret was revealed. We all surrounded him, right there in the shower room, a minyan of levelheaded Jewish boys, and we gazed at his Christianity with a sense of discovery and amazement.

"What happened, Johnny?" someone asked.

"Did they make a mistake?" said another.

"How can you pee with a thing like that?"

"Do you need special underwear?"

Poor Johnny just stammered and shriveled in the glare of the spotlight, until Coach Klezak came to his rescue. "He's Catholic, boys," the coach said. "Now put your damn eyes back into your sockets and get dressed."

So Christians *were* different, in the most basic of ways. And even the children acted accordingly.

That fact bothered William Cartan, editor of the village's main newspaper, the *Skokie News*. "It's about time somebody brought the ugly subject into the open," Cartan said. "Some of the stories I've heard have made me wonder about the future of the kids in our community," he wrote.

Cartan, it seems, had interviewed public school teachers and a Skokie official and a rabbi and a Christian priest, and what he was told disturbed him. "The most alarming part of it all," said Cartan, was the fact that Jewish students stood "aloof" from social, athletic, and other school functions. Jewish kids stayed with their own, he said, "in isolation on the school ground, refusing to mingle with other students." Teachers, he said, were "bending over backward" in a "desperate effort" to help Jewish kids better integrate themselves into school life.

But parents, he said, had a role to play, too. What should one make, he asked, of the Jewish family who "refused to allow its children to speak to neighboring Jewish children because the parents (who'd assimilated to the Christian-American popular culture) hung a wreath on the family door during Christmas"? What should one make, he wondered, of a young Jewish boy, inexperienced in the ways of the world, who nonetheless casually told him "the Catholics are no good"? What should one do, he said, with the "many reliable reports of other families which are spreading seeds of hatred in the neighborhood against Jews"? And what should one say to the non-Jewish kid who stood in a schoolyard and within earshot of teachers proclaimed with aversion: "I guess we won't be using pigskin for footballs much longer"?

Cartan concluded that Skokie was facing a "bloodless battle of neighbor against neighbor" that was splitting the community into different camps. He wrote those words in 1955, and I suppose that, six years later, things hadn't changed much, that the Christmas creche crisis was just the latest, and most pronounced, skirmish between the religions.

My determination to end that skirmish, to make Suzie happy by finding Jesus, to understand why she cared for him dearly all led to considerable reflection on my part. But apart from my knowledge of Johnny Murphy's secret (and apart from my friendship with Suzie, of course), I didn't have much to go on.

I looked to my family and neighbors for guidance, but it didn't help.

"A Jew gone wrong" is what Grandpa Abe said of Jesus. "The source of all our troubles" is how Grandma Emma put it. Mrs. Zimmer, who lived on our block, wouldn't let "goyim" into her house, so she didn't have much to say. And Mrs. Levy, whose teenage son, Stevie, was quite the hunk, wasn't too useful, either: she believed Christians were evil and wouldn't speak of them, but for a promise to throw herself through a plate-glass window if Stevie were ever to date a shiksa.

My parents, I think, were gentler than most on this issue, if equally clueless. I don't imagine they cared much for Jesus. But they did abide my seeing Suzie (small chance, they figured, that marriage would flow from our childhood tryst). And when they did on occasion speak of Christ—"Jesus Christ, honey, are we having meat loaf again for dinner?"—it was out of context, nonjudgmental, and, alas, totally useless as a source of insight into what made him tick.

So I gathered additional data from empirical evidence found elsewhere.

I knew, for instance, that Christians prayed on Sundays, for the Christian stores opened late that day, or never opened at all. I knew that Christians prayed while kneeling, because my mother shrieked and nearly fainted when she once caught my little sister talking to God, hands clasped, in a bedtime genuflection. Thanks to television, the movies, and art museums, I knew what Jesus looked like, the long hair, beard, and robes and all. And, of course, it was common knowledge in the community that Jesus sanctioned bacon, ham, and barbecue spareribs.

It was Christmastime, however, that gave me the most exposure to Christ, for even Skokie celebrated his birth. Christian homes exploded with wonderful displays of ornaments and lights, and believe it or not, even a few Jewish households joined in the fun, with Hanukkah bushes and the like. But I remember Christmas mostly for the annual East Prairie Christmas Pageant, and from it I discovered the spirit and beauty and vision of what I think moved Suzie so.

We all had to participate in the pageant, regardless of religion. Some Jewish kids objected to the exercise, but I loved it, mostly because of the music. The carols were lovely and captivating and mysterious, and I really enjoyed singing them. "Silent Night" and "God Rest Ye Merry Gentlemen" were my favorites, and when the combined third-, fourth-, and fifth-grade chorus sang out, fortissimo: "Remember Christ our Savior was born on Christmas Day," I shivered and tears filled my eyes, so strong was the pull of the song.

The words, to me, were incidental, and even meaningless, though their utterance did, I suppose, amount to blasphemy and sacrilege in a Jewish sort of way. If I had any doubt about that fact, Grandpa Abe set me straight when he walked out of the pageant, the one and only time he attended, unable to stomach the heresy before him. Afterward, he lectured me on the dangers of assimilation, quoting his namesake, Rabbi Abraham

Isaac Kook, the chief rabbi of Palestine, who warned that "Jewry in the diaspora has no real foundation and is disintegrating at an alarming rate." "History teaches," Abe said, "and history has repeatedly shown us that a generation practicing assimilation and ignorance of its faith is easy prey to spiritual as well as physical extinction."

Assimilation, however, wasn't the issue in my search for Jesus. Suzie Louise Anderson was. And however ignorant I may have been in the ways of Christ and of Christians, I knew that my cause was worthy and my mission just. *Deus vult!* cried the crusaders. The time for action was upon us.

The posse I'd gathered to search for the missing Christ child consisted of me, Norman-Meyer, Eva Singer, and Shlomo Rappoport, Reb Rappoport's twelve-year-old son. Eva consented to join us because I asked her to and she liked me. Shlomo agreed only because I paid him. He was his father's son, and the bribe was exacting—two and a half bucks, a Ron Santo baseball card, a package of root beer fizzies, and the two latest Captain America comic books. But the payoff, I figured, was large, for Shlomo's participation gave our endeavor the color and cover of rabbinical license.

Shlomo Rappoport was a pint-size version of his father, the rebbe. Barely five feet tall, he wore the *payos*, or side locks, of the most reverential, and he dressed, like his father, in white shirts with black jacket and pants. His complexion was pallid and pasty from an absence of sunlight. And his nature, to my mind, was unsophisticated and biting, from an absence of socialization. Shlomo went to yeshiva, a private religious school. So his circle of contacts was limited, and his sense of his place in the world narrow.

Shlomo didn't much like people, let alone Christians or Jesus. He was most comfortable hanging around his father, engaging in Socratic-like dialogues about arcane issues of Jewish law and tradition.

"Papa," Shlomo would ask, "who is the luckiest man in the world?"

"Adam," Reb Rappoport would reply.

"And why, Papa, was Adam the luckiest?"

"Because, my young son, in the words of a sage, he had no mother-in-law."

"Papa," Shlomo would ask, "who is bound for heaven?"

"To heaven shall go the devout," Reb Rappoport would say.

"And who, Papa, shall go to hell?"

"In the words of the Talmud, he who follows his wife's counsel tumbles into hell, my son."

Shlomo originally balked when I asked him to join our enterprise. "The goys are no good," he said. "They're all a bunch of anti-Semites. Why do you want to help them?"

"How much do you want?" I asked.

After a half hour's haggling, our arrangement was struck, and the young Rappoport was on board.

My strategy was straightforward. A Jew had kidnapped Jesus. So among Jews we would look. We would canvass the neighborhood, knocking on everyone's door, asking questions, looking for anything circumstantial or direct that might put us onto the trail of Christ. With hard labor and luck, we would find baby Jesus and return him to the Village Hall manger by Christmas.

In the area we became known as the Jesus Rescue Committee. Here's how we worked:

The four of us gathered at my house each day after school. We put on white armbands with the Star of David drawn in the cloth so as to distinguish ourselves from other law enforcement authorities. Norman-Meyer suggested that each of us take on specific tasks, so as to better coordinate the investigation. Shlomo, we decided, would ring all the doorbells or knock on the doors and convey our initial greetings, according to a script that I'd written. "Hello, Mrs. Cohen," he'd say, bowing respectfully. "How are you today? May God bless your Jewish household and your lovely daughter, Rivka."

That having been done, I would take over as official group spokesman.

"Mrs. Cohen," I would say, "we are looking for Jesus. As you probably know, he was kidnapped from the nativity scene at Village Hall. We think that a Jew did it. Do you have any information as to his whereabouts?"

Then I'd describe the baby Jesus as best as I could—sixteen inches tall, three pounds in weight, with outstretched plaster arms—and I would query as to whether my interviewee had crossed paths with such a figure.

Eva was designated note taker, and she'd stand beside me as I spoke, pencil and paper in hand, writing down anything relevant that anyone said. She was also our official interpreter, and helped me out when Yiddish, not English, seemed the more appropriate language of interrogation.

As for Norman-Meyer, due to his bulk, he was our bodyguard. Given the fact that the theft of Christ had put the community on edge, we figured it was only prudent to care for security. So Norman-Meyer, armed with a baseball bat and a twelve-ounce water pistol, walked shotgun as we marched single file from house to house. And he protected our flank when we interviewed suspects.

As the days passed and our work continued, the reception was mixed.

"What on earth are you kids doing?" Mrs. Liechtenstein said. "What kind of a thing is this for Jews to be messing with?"

Mr. Zimmer added. "Let the Gentiles handle it. It's their business, not ours."

"*Hosti amol gezen Yezusn, Misez Rabinovitch?* Have you seen Jesus, Mrs. Rabinowitch?" Eva asked.

"*Yoyzl? Oy vay, ikh zol nisht derlebn!* Jesus? Oy vay, I should never live so long!" the old lady replied.

Even my grandpa Abe looked unkindly upon our endeavor. "Bobby," he said, "I know you're fond of this little girl Suzie. But this thing that you're doing, this search for Jesus, it brings shame upon our family. Jews should look out for their own. We've got enough troubles without having to look out for the goyim."

Not everyone felt that way, and a few of our neighbors welcomed our efforts. Bonnie Goodstein, the Oakton Street baker's wife, gave us cookies each evening to nourish our search. Her husband, Mannie, who'd later arrange the Ping-Pong-ball drop, took out an ad in the *Skokie Life* offering a year's worth of onion bagels to anyone providing information that would lead to the recovery of Jesus alive.

Rabbi Green, our Hebrew-school teacher, was also supportive, promising to post a handbill at the synagogue soliciting information about the abduction of Christ. (The handbill, we later found out, was removed by an angry member of the Temple Shalom sisterhood.) And Irving Weiner, who ran the neighborhood drugstore, said that what we were doing was a mitzvah, a religious duty. "The Torah teaches us, 'And you shall love your neighbor as yourself,'" he said. "Seems to me Christians are our neighbors, and Jesus is important to them. You kids are doing the right thing, and you should be proud of yourselves."

The problem was, we weren't getting much in the way of information, and Christmas was fast approaching. The only lead we had was a report, by Mrs. Berkowitz, that she'd heard a neighbor's dog barking plaintively at 10:15 on the evening of the abduction. The dog belonged to Sollie Shulman, a local automobile dealer, who lived near Village Hall. We interviewed Sollie, who cooperated fully, and examined the dog, Pickles, who had since become pregnant. After consulting Pickles's veterinarian, we constructed a time line for Pickles's condition, and the best we could figure was that Pickles got dilled on the night Jesus vanished. Interesting, to be sure. But useless as far as providing a lead to the villain who kidnapped Christ.

By the time Christmas Eve came, our effort had failed miserably. Jesus was still missing and most surely dead. And there was no substitute, for Village Hall officials had pointedly left his manger empty as an act of defiance against the perpetrator who'd snatched him. Christians and Jews eyed each other with uncommon levels of suspicion. And Suzie was crestfallen, grateful for my effort to find her Lord, but convinced that, without baby Jesus, her Christmas would collapse like a building that had lost its foundation, and her yuletide prayers, whatever they were, would remain unanswered. Suzie didn't even go to church for midnight mass that evening, despite entreaties from her parents, who went without her. She stayed home alone, saddened and teary eyed, an orphan of a missing Son of God, not quite able to comprehend her loss.

I don't know what Suzie prayed for that Christmas of 1961. But she and her family would move, unexpectedly, to their farm in Wisconsin as soon as the winter had ended. I wondered whether that move was the answer to some Christmastime plea to the heavens on her part. Perhaps the trauma of losing Jesus was too much for Suzie's sweet heart to handle. Or maybe it was the realization that Christians and Jews, and she and I, were, in fact, different; that differences can sometimes create confusion, suspicion, hostility, and unpleasantness; and that all of those things had stirred her, perhaps, to ask the Almighty to take her away to a simpler place, to a place where she'd be among her own.

Before her departure, Suzie and I carried on as good friends. We spent the remainder of the winter doing what we'd always done: talking, playing, walking to school, keeping to ourselves. We didn't speak much about what had happened that Christmas, once it was over. And the abduction of Jesus and the events surrounding it never managed to taint my memory of Suzie Louise Anderson, my first love.

And today, when I think of her, what I see first in the eye of my mind is her long, golden hair and her ocean-blue eyes, staring out at me from her living room window that Christmas Eve night in 1961. She was gazing at me lovingly, as if by my presence the sadness above her had lifted, at least for the moment. And she watched, with the hint of a smile breaking her lips, as I stood there alone, on the porch of her house, holding a candle, and singing—to her, not to Jesus—the beautiful strains of a seasonal carol whose melody God, whether Christian or Jewish, must surely have written:

> Silent night, holy night,
> All is calm, all is bright
> 'Round yon virgin mother and child
> Holy infant so tender and mild,
> Sleep in heavenly peace.
> Sleep in heavenly peace.

CHAPTER 7

Aunt Jemima

Leroy Dalcourt was the first black man I'd ever met. I was nine. He was thirty-three. I was the son of a hardworking, middle-class salesman from the West Side of Chicago, a man who had managed to buy for his family a two-story house with a barbecue and a willow tree in a mainly Jewish and altogether white suburb. Leroy was the son of a hardworking Louisiana sharecropper who owned his dignity, but not much else.

Leroy Dalcourt grew up near St. Martinville, in a knotholed wooden shack of a home on the south Louisiana prairie. His father worked the sugarcane fields, and as a young man, so did Leroy, although come wintertime he'd head over to Lafayette, to the big city, where he found construction jobs and carpentry skills and a few extra dollars. Leroy married at eighteen and had two kids, and his papa, wise to the ways of the South, told his son to join the great migration north, to Chicago, to the promised land of opportunity. So in 1951, at the age of twenty-three, Leroy did just that.

Leroy got hired as a warehouseman and odd jobber at Chicago Brady Motorfreight, the south-side trucking company that happened to employ my father. Leroy and his family found housing where they could, first in a one-room tenement hovel near his place of business, and later more spacious quarters in a tired and creaky two-and-a-half-room west-side apartment.

The west-side residence sat atop a grocery store on a block where Jews had once lived but which they had mostly abandoned. A wooden mezuzah—a thin, rectangular case with religious Scripture inside—was still affixed to the doorpost of Leroy's new place when he moved in. Jews mark their homes with mezuzahs to symbolize God's presence, and the previous tenants had left theirs behind, figuring, probably, that theirs was a Jewish apartment, that Jews would always live there, so God, and the mezuzah, had better stay put. Leroy didn't know what to make of the thing. His wife called it their lucky charm.

Leroy met my dad, Jacob, on the Brady Motorfreight loading dock. Jacob was handling bills of lading. Leroy was handling eighty-pound boxes. Their relationship was polite but perfunctory: Leroy loaded trucks and built warehouse pallets; my dad wore a tie and hustled the streets. When their paths crossed, communication was limited to head nods or occasional banter. It was the kind of relationship two people have who know that they'll never be friends, but who figure that, all things considered, they might as well be civil.

"Hey, Leroy, howya doin'?"

"Mr. Bakalchuk, doin' just fine, thank you very much."

"How about those White Sox, eh?"

"Yessir, Mr. Bakalchuk, those White Sox doin' just fine, just fine."

And thus, as the years passed, in this way did the two men develop a certain measure of familiarity, trust, and respect. So in the late summer of 1961, when my dad got a bonus and decided to finish the basement of our home, Leroy, who was a freelance carpenter, got the job. Leroy had worked on the homes of others at Brady, and came to the job highly recommended.

"Leroy," my dad said, "can you come on up to my home this Sunday to survey the basement with me?"

"Sure thing, Mr. Bakalchuk," Leroy said. "Just tell me how to get there and when."

Thus did Leroy Dalcourt have cause, for the first time, to enter Skokie, and to visit my block.

To say he was nervous about the trip would fairly assess his condition. Leroy knew that Skokie was a white village, and he generally preferred to steer clear of all-white locations. It was dangerous, he knew, to enter a white man's plantation alone. That was the case in the South. And nothing he'd seen since he'd moved to Chicago suggested that things were much different there. Chicago was, in fact, the country's single most segregated city. Blacks stayed with blacks. Whites stayed with whites. And anyone who roamed, by mistake or design, into enemy territory did so at their own risk. That's just the way it was.

"Leroy," his wife said, anxiously picking the skin of her thumb, "are you sure you ought to be goin' to that place by yourself? Lord knows what kind of neighborhood it is, what kind of people are there."

"C'est bon," Leroy said tentatively. "It'll be okay. Mr. Bakalchuk's a nice man, a real nice man, and besides, I like carpentry work and we need the extra money. So don't you worry, you."

But just to be safe, before leaving to visit my home for the first time, Leroy put on a freshly ironed white shirt and a tie and a jacket. It was, after all, a Sunday, the Lord's day, and he wanted to look good to make a favorable impression on the Bakalchuk household. And, while walking to his car, Leroy decided to drop into church, for what could be lost by praying for God's grace on this day, as he prepared to drive north to my house?

"Dear Lord," Leroy said, "please bless and protect me as I travel into the other side of your town."

Leroy crossed himself, looked up toward the heavens, drew a

deep breath, crossed himself again, and said, "Amen." Then he left the church, got into his car, and headed toward the Edens Expressway, to the Touhy Avenue exit, for Skokie.

A black man was the last thing poor old Mordechai Rappoport had ever expected to see in our neighborhood. And, if truth be told, he had never, in his seventy-five years, ever seen a black man up close before, let alone talked with one. For the better part of a decade, the aged Orthodox rabbi with the wide-brimmed hat and the Moses-like beard had wandered the streets of Skokie, cane in one hand, large, round metal container for donations in the other. He shuffled to and fro across his suburban realm, day in and day out—resting, of course, on the Sabbath—knocking on Jewish doors, haranguing the likes of Sofie Milstein and Ida Zimmer with unsolicited but nevertheless sagacious commentary on Sofie's latest weight gain or Ida's summertime habit of wearing pink halters and painting her toenails red. And, having beleaguered his victims to the point of intemperance, Reb Rappoport, for the most part, succeeded in his mission, which was, of course, the collection of money to further promote and propagate his favorite Jewish cause, which was, of course, Reb Mordechai Rappoport.

His was honest work, hard work, and work that the rebbe found immensely rewarding. And with the exception of an occasional bee sting or a barking dog or an impertinent elderly biddy, old Rappoport felt entirely safe while making his rounds in the village. The territory was familiar, and he was accustomed to the light, as it were, for he was among his own.

So the sight of a black man caught his eye, and it stuck there like a speck of dirt.

"Oy," thought the rebbe, who grew quite agitated when he saw Leroy. "What is this? Why is this man on my sidewalk? Coming in my direction? He is an outsider, and he doesn't belong here. He can only cause trouble."

The rebbe turned anxious, and even somewhat scared.

Leroy had parked his car down the block from my house, and he was trying to find his bearings when he noticed Reb Rappoport. To Leroy the man looked hoary and foreboding, like a ghost. The rebbe reminded Leroy of the Cajun swamp rats of his youth, the gnarly old men with the long, scraggly beards and beaver-skin caps who, just for the kicks of it, sent buckshot over the heads of the black Creole kids who fished in the bayous of the Atchafalaya basin. This was no bayou, this place called Skokie, and there were no swamp rats here. And Leroy was no kid. But he knew, nonetheless, that it would probably be better not to provoke this strange-looking fellow, if at all possible.

Leroy got out of his car and began walking down the block in search of my house. He was visibly edgy, Leroy was, now that he'd left the safety of his vehicle, a lone black man on this white suburban street. Nobody but the strange old man with the cane and the beard was around to threaten him, but Leroy felt vulnerable nonetheless, as if he were on stage, with the whole white world watching, scrutinizing judgmentally, every twitch of his body. He stuck his hands in his pockets and stared at the ground as he walked ahead. And he tried to find fortitude in his favorite hymn, "Onward Christian Soldiers," which he whistled softly to himself.

Reb Rappoport stood there on the sidewalk as Leroy approached, not knowing what to think. To the rabbi, this black man, who was of moderate height and really quite thin, seemed as big as Goliath and just as imposing, like a hulking, shadowy alien object eclipsing the sun.

Reb Rappoport silently watched the black man, who was now just yards in front of him. The rebbe's heart ran with adrenaline now. "Dear God," he thought, "what shall I do?" His frail old chest heaved in and out, and hoarse little guttural croaks filled his throat as he searched for air. He was visibly losing control. His left hand began to quiver, and the coins in the can he was holding there rattled and clinked in a pathetic little cry of alarm that nobody but the black man and the rebbe could hear, for there was nobody else within earshot of the encounter between them.

Leroy, already on edge, was startled by the gyrations of his adversary. "Lord Jesus," Leroy thought, "what if this man dies of a heart attack? Lord Jesus, that's all I need." So Leroy did what he'd promised himself he wouldn't do: he spoke to the rebbe.

"Uh, are you okay, sir?" Leroy asked, concerned about the effect his presence was having on the old man.

The rebbe's face tightened. Suddenly, Reb Rappoport conceived of a plan. He leaned on his cane and steadied himself as best he could. Then he looked at the black man.

"*Nisht* English!" he barked. "*Ikh ken nisht redn kan* English! *Ikh red nor Yidish!*"

Well, you can imagine the effect that this unanticipated cacophony of sound had on poor Leroy, who was, after all, from south Louisiana, where French was first, English second, and Yiddish never was and never would be. His eyes ballooned with astonishment when he heard the man speak, and his brows hopped so high that they nearly jumped off his face. What kind of tongue did this strange man possess? What in the name of the Lord was he saying?

Leroy felt as if he had to pee. The man's foreign utterance just reinforced his jitters. Never before in his life had he heard such talk. Mr. Bakalchuk never spoke to him that way. What kind of place was this village called Skokie? What kind of people lived here?

Leroy stood there now, immobilized by apprehension, toe to toe with Mordechai Rappoport. The rebbe was similarly afflicted. So the two men, from opposite ends of the planet, stared at each other, transfixed, unable to extricate themselves from the predicament before them.

Reb Rappoport, by divine intervention he later would say, moved next. *"Nisht* English!" the rebbe shouted, his voice lifted less by mettle than by out-and-out panic. *"Ikh ken nisht redn kan* English! *Ikh red nor Yidish!"*

"Lordie Lord," Leroy said, flustered. "Mister, with all due respect, I don't know where you from, and I don't wanna know, me. So I'll be on my way now, if you don't mind." And Leroy scampered past Reb Rappoport as quickly as he could, inadvertently bumping, quite forcefully, the rebbe's shoulder in the process of escaping. And he continued on his way, in search of my house, hoping beyond hope that the rebbe would stay in his place and let him be. Which is, of course, exactly what happened, for now it was Mordechai Rappoport who had to pee.

Others, of course, saw the black man that day, as he strolled past our homes on the neighborhood sidewalk that led him directly to Jacob Bakalchuk's house.

When Mrs. Milstein saw Leroy through her living room picture window, she told her young grandson, Barry, to wait a while before going outside to play, and she directed Matzoh Ball, her miniature French poodle, to stand guard at the door.

When Mrs. Zimmer saw the man, she reached for the phone and dialed the police to report a suspicious person. And the police, on the basis of Mrs. Zimmer's description, dispatched a cruiser to check out a lone black male seen wandering on Jarvis Street between Crawford and East Prairie Road, in a jacket and tie.

When Fay Margules, who'd been at the market, caught sight of the man from her car down the block, she gathered her groceries and scurried into her house, trying to avoid the black man seeing her. Once inside, Fay dialed up her best friend, Irma

Schwab, who lived down the road. "Irma," she said, "there's a *schvartzer* outside. Close your drapes and lock up your doors."

And when Joseph Ashkenaz, Norman-Meyer's father, glanced at the black man, whom he happened to see through his bedroom window, his muscles tensed and his pupils dilated, and he reached for his rifle and glared at the stranger from the safety of his home. "It's enough that I have to put up with you and your mother," he said to his son, "and now this, a *schvartzer* roaming around loose on the block?"

When Jacob Bakalchuk finally saw Leroy, he opened the door to his home and let him in.

"Hello, Leroy," my dad said cheerfully. "Come on in. Did you have any trouble finding the place?"

"No sir, Mr. Bakalchuk," Leroy said. "No problem. Doin' just fine, just fine. Now where is that basement of yours?"

Leroy Dalcourt may have been the first black man I'd ever met, but he was not the first black person I'd ever encountered. There was, first of all, Aunt Jemima.

Aunt Jemima was hostess at Aunt Jemima's Kitchen ("America's Favorite Pancakes!") at 4700 Dempster Road, in the heart of Skokie. The restaurant promised "real old-fashioned southern charm," thirty-seven kinds of delicious pancakes, and a setting in which, according to an advertisement, you could "almost hear mockingbirds sing—almost catch a scent of magnolia in the air!"

For the first five years of my life, Aunt Jemima's was home away from home. We'd eat there every Sunday morning, without question, drawn to the place by the genteel nature of its hostess and the buck-ninety-five specials. As a toddler, I tasted my first bites of solid food at Aunt Jemima's: silver-dollar pancakes, wrapped with butter and soaked through with maple syrup.

I really believed back then—how, living in Skokie, would I know differently?—that the overweight woman with the big black cheeks *was* Aunt Jemima. She *said* she was Aunt Jemima, and that's what we called her. She *looked* like Aunt Jemima, adorned as she was in an apron and checkered dress with a matching bandanna wrapped around her head. The local newspaper, in a feature about the place, printed her picture and *identified* her as Aunt Jemima. And she *talked* as an Aunt Jemima would, always greeting us at the door with a heartfelt "Well, hi there, y'all" and a convincing smile.

"Hi, Aunt Jemima!" I'd say, with genuine enthusiasm, upon seeing her each Sunday.

"Well, hello there, sugar," she'd reply, reaching out and tickling my belly till I giggled to her satisfaction.

"Are you hungry this fine mornin', lil' Bobby?" she'd ask me.

"I'm gonna eat a buhzillion pancakes today!" I'd reply.

"Well, save some for your mama and papa, you hear me?" And she'd seat us at our favorite table in the Garden Room, which was made out in French Quarter style, and fuss all over us until we'd had our fill.

We'd often come to Aunt Jemima's with my grandparents Abe and Emma. Aunt Jemima thought Grandpa Abe was just the cutest little old thing on earth. "Mr. Abe," Aunt Jemima would say, "my, you're looking good this morning. Miss Emma, you better watch out now, lest I take that man away from you!" And Emma would shoot a cold Romanian gaze back at Aunt Jemima, who never noticed such things, and Abe would blush with discomfort and order hot tea.

I liked Aunt Jemima. And I liked her restaurant. And to me and the legions of others who ate there, Aunt Jemima's embodied the South, and Aunt Jemima, or the nameless woman who played her, did a lot to define the way each of us perceived black women who lived in the South. Or, for that matter, the way we perceived black women who lived almost anywhere.

Then there was Charlotte. Charlotte once lived in the South. In Birmingham, Alabama. She moved to Chicago in the early fifties to stay with her older sister, who'd moved to the city during the war. Charlotte resided in Chicago's South Side. But six days a week she commuted north, ninety minutes by train and by bus, to our house, and to others around us, to work as a cleaning lady. She was the second black woman I knew, next to Aunt Jemima. And the first whom my little sister had met. "She was big and fat and smelled like ammonia, and I was afraid of her." That's how my sister recalls Charlotte. For my part, I believed Charlotte and Aunt Jemima were sisters. Only Charlotte didn't serve pancakes. She did laundry instead.

But of all the black folk in our suburban shtetl, Leroy was unquestionably my favorite. I was the first little Jewish kid he'd ever met, and he took a serious liking to me, and I to him. I hung out around Leroy whenever I could, watching, with a nine year old's admiration, as he transformed our basement from a concrete hole in the ground to a wood-paneled, floor-tiled family room complete with a wet bar. He worked with wood and saws and lathes and hammers—a little boy's wish list of things to play with—and he let me help out every once in a while.

"Put that nail there, you," he'd say in his peculiar south-Louisiana style of speech. And I'd happily hammer the thing as directed. "Bon, Tee Robert," he'd say. "Well done, little Robert."

I remember especially Leroy's hands. They were a laborer's hands, big and calloused from a lifetime of cutting and pulling and hauling and moving. And I remember his palms, and how white they were when compared to the rest of his body. And I wondered why that was so, why Leroy had palms that looked like mine, but the rest of his body didn't.

Leroy worked at our house two days a week, Fridays and Saturdays, for five months straight. The rest of the time, including the late shift on Sundays, he labored at the docks of Brady Motorfreight, which was a twenty-four-hour, seven-day-a-week operation. Sometimes Leroy slept over at our place, so he wouldn't have to make the long commute south to the West Side, only to return north again early the next morning. He slept in a cot in the basement, with sawdust and wood paneling and linoleum tiles. And he ate there alone.

Grandpa Abe, though usually the most civil and fair-minded of men, didn't much like the fact that Leroy was staying overnight at his daughter's home. "It just isn't done," he'd say to my mom, shaking his head. "What will the neighbors think, a *schvartzer* sleeping overnight in a Jewish home? It just isn't done."

Nothing untoward happened, of course. And by year's end, Leroy was gone and our basement completed. My dad was pleased with the work Leroy had done. And my mother was glad he had finally left, for she was often left alone in the house with Leroy while my dad was at work, and, to be honest, that made her feel uncomfortable. My mother didn't dislike Leroy. It's just that she never talked much with him. He did his work in the basement. She stayed upstairs in the kitchen. When my mom did have occasion to speak with Leroy, she called him "Leroy." When Leroy replied, he called her "Mistress."

During the autumn that Leroy worked in our basement, Skokie underwent what people later called "the adjustment." It had nothing to do with Leroy. It had everything to do with Morton Silver—the village *mohel*—and a man by the name of Willie Watson.

Morton, who lived on my block, made a living—and in those baby boom days a very good one—performing one of the most joyful, honored, and delicate of Jewish rituals: the

Covenant of Circumcision. Morton's mandate—and, I should add, he pursued the directive with considerable humility—was divinely conceived: from Gen. 17:10–14: And God told the Is-raelites: "This is My Covenant which you shall keep: that every male among you shall be circumcised, and that shall be the sign of the Covenant between Me and you. And that at the age of eight days every male among you shall be circumcised through-out the generations. And the uncircumcised male shall be cut off from his people, for he has broken My Covenant."

It is said that the Jews are a stiff-necked people, with minds of their own. Get two Jews together, the saying goes, and you'll get ten opinions. But on one thing the Jews are clear: the covenant is serious stuff, and you don't want to break it. Jewish law states, "Behold how gladsome is circumcision that not even the Sabbath defers it!" Clearly, then, there is no room for com-promise here. You have but one course if you are a Jewish male: lie down, don't move, and submit to the knife so you don't get cut off from your people.

Thus did Morton Silver prosper. But circumcision was just his craft. His passion lay elsewhere, in the realm of politics.

In looks and demeanor, Morton didn't exactly fit the para-digm of a beat-era social activist. His wife, Reva, a Lithuanian Jew who had survived the death camps, called him her *kleyntshiker git hartziger mentsh, vi a sove mit a lise kop*, her "little old sweet-hearted, bald-headed hoot owl." Hardly the stuff of a fire-brand. Indeed, the moniker made some sense. Morton had the thinning gray crown of fifty-plus years, with a round, flat face, wide-open eyes, a beak of a nose, and ears that, although not quite owlish, did predispose the man to listen rather than speak. He was exceedingly intelligent and deferentially polite, and de-spite the public nature of his profession—circumcisions, after all, are performed on stage, as it were, amid considerable pomp and celebration—Morton shunned the limelight, eschewing the honor and glory rightfully due a *mohel* of his caliber. He was, in short, reclusive by nature, and not the type of man to trumpet ideology on the local street corner. But make no mistake about it: Morton had principles. He knew what was right, and in his own quiet way, he acted on his beliefs.

Morton was born in Chicago, the only son of a German immigrant, Rabbi Yitzhak Silver, who ran a small synagogue in the "Poor Jew's Quarter" on Maxwell Street, in the city's Near West Side. Yitzhak, above everything, wanted to raise his son in the image of God, and to Yitzhak doing so meant that his son, above all, must become, in God's eyes and in the eyes of his children on earth, a decent and good-hearted man. Every father, I suppose, wants the same for his child. But the serendipity of Morton's birth, for a religious man like Yitzhak, underscored the mission: Morton was born on the eve of Simchas Torah, the most joyous of Jewish festivals, which celebrates the end of the annual cycle of weekly readings from the Torah, or Five Books of Moses.

Under normal circumstances, Simchas Torah calls for profound and unbridled merriment, an occasion, in the words of the scholar Hayyim Schauss, in which "old, pious men, with long cloaks and gray beards, cavort about and sing, and act as if a sudden, wild joy had taken complete possession of them." Imagine, then, the revelry surrounding Morton's birth. Yitzhak had found profound significance in the timing of the event. His child, for sure, would be blessed. The boy would be marked by God to do good in the world. In short, Yitzhak was simply beside himself with happiness, which was a cause for extraordinary celebration.

So on the day that Morton was born, once the sun had set, officially starting the holiday, and once his congregation had gathered for prayer, Yitzhak collected his son, barely twelve hours old, and lovingly draped him in the warmth of a prayer shawl. And he cradled the baby in the crook of one arm. And to anoint the moment, he placed the scrolls of the Torah in his other arm, and buoyed by the shouts and cheers of assembled worshipers, Yitzhak and Morton and the Scriptures of the Pentateuch paraded around the small sanctuary a full seven times, as custom demanded. And with each procession, the "hurrahs" and the *mazel tovs* grew louder and louder, and Yitzhak whooped and shrieked with abandon until he could barely breathe. And the congregation joined in, and all pretext of decorum was lost. It was, they said later, as if God himself had loosened his tie and appeared in their midst and danced through their ranks with the frenzy of a whirling dervish.

As Morton grew up, Yitzhak took care to ensure that his son understood the meaning of his birth, and its connection to the precepts of Judaism.

"Morton," his father would say, "the essence of Judaism, the essence of the Torah, can be summed up in one word, and that word is *chesed*, or kindness. And *chesed* means simply this—and I want you always to remember—*chesed* means compassion. Do you understand? Compassion. It means that you must not do unto others what you wouldn't want others to do unto you. It means that you must love your neighbor as yourself."

Morton remembered his father's words, and he deeply believed in them. And as he grew older, he tried as best he could to give life to their meaning. At first, Morton thought he'd become a rabbi. "What is more decent or kind than preaching the Torah to our people?" he reasoned. But halfway through his rabbinical training, Morton thought better. Religious studies bored him. They struck him as entirely too pedantic, especially then, in the depression, when soup kitchens, foreclosures, and joblessness seemed to marginalize the Talmud, the great body of Jewish law, which he had been studying.

"If a hungry, out-of-work Jew wants to eat a piece of ham, or wants to mix some milk with his meat because that's the only food a soup kitchen offers, I'm certainly not going to get in his way," Morton told his father, Yitzhak, in explaining his decision to forego the rabbinate.

"My God, you've become a communist!" Yitzhak responded, heartbroken.

Morton instead turned his mind toward medicine. That trade, he believed, was the most compassionate. He entered medical school with the intention of becoming a pediatrician. "What is more decent or kind than healing the children?" he figured.

Then the war came. And Hitler. And Morton's course was clear. He dropped out of medical school, joined the army, and served in Europe as a surgeon's assistant.

Morton met his wife, Reva, in a refugee camp in 1945. She was liberated from Auschwitz at age twenty-one, and was thirteen years his junior. Morton looked after her health, and the two fell in love. They married when the dark patches vanished beneath Reva's eyes, and her hair again breathed and was able to flow as it once had to the small of her back. Reva wanted it that way. She wanted to be a pretty bride.

After the war, Morton brought Reva to Chicago. They lived for a time in a West Side apartment, then moved north, to Skokie, to a home of their own on my block. Morton became a *mohel.* "What is more decent or kind, with millions of our people dead, than to sanctify the Lord's covenant with a newly born baby boy?" he thought. And with Reva unable to bear children—a cruel gift from Auschwitz—Morton considered himself doubly obliged to surround himself with the next generation of Israel.

In addition, he started—in his own purposeful, simple way—to pursue other endeavors, which in his estimation fulfilled the mandate of his birth, the mandate of Simchas Torah and of *chesed*, of compassion and kindness. He subscribed first of all to the New York edition of the *Jewish Daily Forward* for he liked the paper's socialist leanings.

Emboldened, he joined the American Civil Liberties Union, for its members were people, he said, "who do the right thing when the right thing is the hard thing to do." He regularly escorted groups of children of local Holocaust survivors to Riverview, the popular amusement park, where he and the kids would delight in the chute-the-chutes and the parachute ride and the House of Horrors. Occasionally, Reva and other survivors would come along, and after some prodding from Morton, they'd hop onto the Bobs, the famous roller coaster, grasp one another's hands, and scream like uncaged lions as the open-air cars looped up and down mountains of rail at breakneck speeds.

Morton also took to writing, and he regularly peppered the *Chicago Tribune* with letters to the editor on a variety of issues, from his desire to "ban the bomb" to the injustices facing blacks. It was, in particular, this issue—civil rights—that captured Morton's attention. "Negroes deserve better, and Jews, of all people, should understand that," he said.

He read Ralph Ellison's *Invisible Man*. He joined the Chicago branch of the National Association for the Advancement of Colored People (NAACP), the first Skokie resident to do so. He contributed fifteen dollars each year to the United Negro College Fund. And, in 1960, he became a member of Housing Opportunities Made Equal (HOME), a Chicago-area organization dedicated to the principle that everybody, regardless of race, religion, or ethnicity, should be able to live wherever they want. It was through HOME that Morton met Willie Watson. And it was through Willie Watson that Morton, the *mohel*, came to the split-level house on Kildare Street in Skokie, and the controversy that lay therein.

CHAPTER 8

The Adjustment

Abe and Emma Yellin met Morton Silver for the first time in 1952, at my circumcision. It was a Chicago West Side affair—nobody had moved to Skokie yet—and it took place in my parents' studio apartment on Karlov Street. The apartment was packed to capacity with family and friends that day, like an overstuffed blintz. Morton, who'd already established a reputation for himself, presided. Reva was there, too, silently grieving, as she always did on such occasions, the fact of her own infertility.

My grandpa had the honor of holding me on his lap while Morton performed the deed. My mom and dad stood beside us, arm in arm, nervously watching. Afterward, when a dribble of wine had dulled my pain and lulled me to sleep, everyone walked over to my grandparents' deli on Roosevelt Road for a celebratory meal. Emma made prune and beef *tsimmes*, the Jews' festive stew.

As the years passed, Morton and Abe and Emma and Reva became friends, though never the best of friends. Reva, of course, was much younger than Emma, and she never cared much for the barbs on Emma's tongue. For her part, Emma could never pierce the wall of Auschwitz that kept all but Morton at arm's length from his wife. And though Morton and Abe were contemporaries, Morton was American born, which Abe figured was the cause of Morton's annoying predilection—annoying to

Abe, at least—for embracing political causes of this or that stripe. "Politics are just a tool, to turn a wise man to a fool." That's how Abe viewed it. Back then, anyway.

Despite their differences, there was a bond between the couples, for they had shared the covenant of my circumcision. So they saw each other regularly, in synagogue or at various West Side community functions. Occasionally, my grandma would have Morton and Reva over for dinner. And the pattern continued in Skokie, once both families had moved there.

In short, Abe and Emma were pretty comfortable with the Silvers. So that closeness was why, in the autumn of 1961, when word got out about Morton and Willie Watson, Emma spoke up at dinner one evening.

The couples had gathered at Morton's house. Reva had prepared brisket. Emma had brought along apple-and-pear compote for dessert. Emma had heard rumors about Willie Watson from Ida Zimmer, who'd heard it from Sally Moskowitz, the banker's wife, who had gotten it from her husband, Eddie, who'd unwittingly handled the shadow mortgage that opened the door to the integration of Skokie.

"Morton," Emma said, an edge to her voice, "have you gone meshuga?"

"Emma, please," Abe said softly.

"Why would you say I'm meshuga?" Morton asked politely.

"This thing with a colored," Emma said. "Is it true? That you're trying to get him to move into Skokie?"

"Emma, please, it's none of our business," Abe said.

"It is true," Morton said, "and, with all due respect, Emma, I don't think it's crazy. The Watsons are good people, and they want to live here. So why shouldn't they?"

Morton looked at Abe. Abe studied a crumb of rye bread that had fallen to the floor.

"Because we should all stay with our own," Emma said. "Jews

with Jews. Goyim with goyim. *Schvartzer* with *schvartzer*. It has always been that way. It's God's way. We should all just stay with our own."

"It is not God's way, Emma," Reva said sharply. "Who are you to judge such things?"

"I know what I know," Emma said.

"You don't know anything," Reva said.

A thick silence ensued. Abe shifted in his chair and twisted the end of his napkin. Morton picked at a piece of meat on his plate.

"Look, Emma," Morton said gently. "The Jews have been treated as second-class citizens for centuries. How many times have people told us, told you, even here in America, to 'stay in your place,' that 'you can't do this' or 'you can't do that,' that 'you can't live here or work there' simply because you're a Jew? How many times have we been victimized simply because of our beliefs, or for that matter, because of the way we look or dress? What does the Holocaust teach us if not the importance of tolerance—more than tolerance—of understanding people, of co-existing with people who are different from you?"

"Those are pretty words," Emma said, "but I know what I know. I know that we moved here to Skokie because the West Side was changing and we wanted to be with our own. And you may not admit it, Morton Silver, but that's why you moved here, too, to get away from the *schvartzers*."

"Emma, please, enough," Abe said.

"We moved here, Emma," Morton said, his voice still respectful and courteous, "because we could afford to buy our own home here. And yes, there are Jews here, and there are survivors here, too, and for Reva that's important. But this is a good place, this village, and if someone, anyone, has the money to purchase a home here, they ought to have that opportunity. They ought to have that right."

"It's a slum, you know," Emma said. "The West Side. Look what they've done to the West Side. It's a slum. You can't even walk down Roosevelt Road anymore. The deli, our deli, was turned into a garbage dump after we let go of it. They ruined our old neighborhood. I just don't want them here. That's all."

Abe, who was a most patient and kind man, found the conversation was now more than he could take. By nature, he didn't like discord, especially among friends. All this talk about Negroes and such made him anxious. The directness of his wife's speech left him embarrassed. These matters are delicate, he thought, and perhaps best left undiscussed. He'd seen his share of *schvartzers*—that's what he called them, too—during his years on the West Side. He'd even hired one to work at the deli, to do dishes and bus tables. He shared his wife's sense of discomfort about black people. And he, too, preferred to be with his own. As for Morton and what he was doing, it was Morton's affair, and only trouble could come of it (although Abe was a fair enough man to know that what Morton was saying was not without some merit). But mostly, now, Abe was tired, and he wanted the conversation to end, so he could go home.

"My dear friends, and my dear wife," Abe said, "the Torah says 'as all faces of people are different, so too are their opinions.' Perhaps we should leave it at that. Morton, Reva, thank you for dinner. Morton, take care of yourself. Emma, it's time to go."

My grandparents rose from the table, saw themselves out the front door, and walked home, leaving Reva still fuming over Emma's behavior, and Morton absorbed in his thoughts about Willie Watson and the house on Kildare Street.

The plan, which was hatched in August 1961, was forthright— if slightly deceptive—and entirely legal: Morton would act as a "nominee" buyer: he'd purchase the house on Kildare Street for himself, as a putative rental home, with down-payment money provided under the table by Willie and Harriet Watson; then, after the deal was struck, after the banker and realtor and seller had thought that they'd sold the place to the esteemed, well-to-do village *mohel*, Morton would transfer title to the Watsons, who'd move in and pick up the mortgage payments for themselves.

The Watsons had been trying to acquire a home in Skokie for months, without success. It's not that they couldn't find a place to their liking. On the contrary. The village had dozens of homes up for sale, and Willie and Harriet found several—including the house on Kildare Street—that they really adored, and could afford. But they were black, Skokie was white, and there were always some problems.

Said the banker: "I'm sorry, your loan has not been approved."

Said the realtor: "Oh, I'm sorry, this place has already been sold. We just haven't removed the 'For Sale' sign yet."

Said the seller: "We don't sell to Negroes."

The Watsons' desire to move to Skokie was not underwritten by lofty political aims. Willie and Harriet were scholars, not activists. They preferred anonymity to the bully pulpit. Geography and convenience were what mattered to them.

Willie had gotten a job as a research scientist at G. D. Searle & Company, the huge pharmaceutical corporation located north of Oakton Street, by the railroad tracks, in the south-central part of Skokie. The Watsons had been living in Chicago's Hyde Park area, near the university, where Willie and Harriet had been graduate students. Willie's Ph.D. was in chemistry. Harriet earned an M.A. in mathematics and teaching. They married upon graduation, and shortly thereafter Willie was hired by Searle.

The commute from Hyde Park was a killer. The mileage was

ample, and traffic was snarly for most of the way. Willie said it was ruining his sense of tranquillity. By the time he'd get home from work for dinner, his nerves were panfried. So the move north made perfect sense. Skokie was safe, the schools there were good, and some of the junior highs were even looking for Negro faculty. Token hires, for sure. But a job was a job, and Harriet, with her credentials, believed she could find a teaching position somewhere in the northern suburbs.

After failing to find a house on their own, Willie called the Chicago office of the NAACP, which put him in touch with HOME, the equal opportunity housing group. HOME contacted Morton Silver, who was a member, and asked if he'd serve as a nominee buyer for a black couple who wanted to move into Skokie. A meeting was arranged in Hyde Park between Morton and Reva and Willie and Harriet. The four of them hit it off well, and a deal was struck over Harriet's homegrown mint tea and some cinnamon raisin kugel that Reva had brought along for the occasion.

The house on Kildare Street was still up for sale, so Morton purchased it without any trouble. Closing was set for September 26. Morton suggested the Watsons move in a week later, on Tuesday, October 3, which happened to be Simchas Torah. "It's the happiest of Jewish holidays," Morton said, "and it symbolizes joy and new beginnings. It's God's will and a bit of serendipity, I think, that you move in on such a day."

The Watsons, who were churchgoing Baptists, agreed.

It was at the closing, as Morton later recounted, that God became capricious and stirred up the batter. The ritualistic signing of documents and conveyance of money took place at the Kildare Street location. Eddie Moskowitz, the banker, had heard from a friend at the Skokie Police Department that Morton was up to some trickery. Morton and HOME organization officers had quietly met with the police a few days before to inform

them that a black couple would soon move to Skokie, and to request police protection if necessary.

"Mr. Silver, are you planning to convey this property to a
colored family?" Eddie asked tentatively.

"Yes, Mr. Moskowitz, that's right, I am," Morton said matter-
of-factly.

Eddie realized he'd been had.

"You son of a bitch," he said. The fulminations that followed
shall not be recounted in detail here. Suffice it to say that Eddie
exhausted his expletive lexicon and darn near exploded from in-
furiation.

There was nothing, in fact, that Eddie could do to abort the
sale, other than what he did: first, stomp out of the house after
closing was finished and physically rip the "For Sale" sign out of
its moorings (the thing had been securely screwed into the
building's brick facade, and its extraction required considerable
muscle power, which Eddie, a weekend golfer of slight repute,
was not believed to possess); and second, alert, as quickly as he
could, the local press.

The article appeared two days later, in the *Skokie Life*.

Morton Silver, a village *mohel*, has purchased a home on the
7400 block of Kildare Street on behalf of a Negro couple, who
intend to move in next Tuesday. The move would make Willie
and Harriet Watson, of Hyde Park, the first colored family to
own property in Skokie.

Mr. Silver said that he and his wife were motivated by
moral compulsion. In a statement, Silver said: "We deeply believe that every American has the right to live where he wants
to and where he can afford to. We do not believe that double
standards should be set up based on race, creed, religion and
place of origin. How can we criticize what is being done in

Mississippi or Alabama if we are practicing a similar type of injustice right here in our own town?"

Mr. Silver, whose wife survived Auschwitz, said that he and his spouse are determined to do what they can to fight evil, bigotry and discrimination. "We believe most profoundly that you must do as you would be done by," Silver said.

Silver added: "We call upon all those who may read this statement to reexamine their own conscience to learn whether they really disagree with what we have done. Let us graciously welcome the Watson family into our midst, rising to this occasion of moral, human and democratic responsibility."

The newspaper went on to report that in response to the imminent integration of Skokie, village trustees had hastily met to discuss the impending crisis. They adopted a decree that said: "The people of the village may rest assured that the constitutional and civil rights of all citizens and property owners, old and new, will be protected. We are confident that all citizens of Skokie share our determination to maintain law and order and to preserve the good name of our community."

The next morning, the 7400 block of Kildare Street was littered with "For Sale" signs—eleven in total. They had bloomed overnight like crocuses stoked by a sudden spring thaw. Circulars appeared in the neighborhood, charging that communism was infiltrating Skokie in the guise of integration. Someone—Morton claimed it was the village—dispatched informational flyers to Kildare Street residents, advising them of the coming adjustment, and providing background information on Willie and Harriet Watson: their names, education, religious affiliation, and employment histories. Harriet said later that "the village had wanted to show we were good niggers."

A posse of well-intentioned clergy—including Sidney

Glickman of Temple Shalom, a Catholic priest, and an Episco-
pal minister—made the rounds of Kildare Street homes, knocking on doors and doing what they could to ease the fears of local
residents. Said Rabbi Glickman: "It was a source of amazement,
shock, and saddened disbelief to me to find some Jews in the
area who could not see a correlation between white antagonism
to the Negroes coming here and the hostility that Jews experienced when they moved into formerly restricted areas of
Skokie."

As the day of the Watsons' arrival approached, Morton decided he'd better take action. He feared for the safety of the Kildare Street house—even with police patrolling the area, who
knew what kind of crazy things people might do?—so he and
Reva packed up some bedding and canned food and bottles of
seltzer and moved into the home, the better to look after the
property until Willie and Harriet settled in. There they were
camped, on Simchas Torah eve, when Norman-Meyer's father,
Joseph Ashkenaz, and a mob of like-minded bigots appeared,
along with the usual curious bystanders.

It was from Norman-Meyer that I first heard about Willie Watson and the house on Kildare Street. He wouldn't have men-
tioned it but for his father, who'd ranted malevolently about the
intrusion, set to take place in just one day; and were it not for
Leroy Dalcourt, the black man who worked in our basement
back then, I don't think Norman-Meyer would have told me
about it at all. But he figured, I guess, that Leroy and I were
friends, and I, as the maven of African culture, needed to know
about relevant developments in the field.

Besides, Norman-Meyer was absolutely taken with Leroy,
and by extension, with other things black. Leroy, like Norman-
Meyer, was different, and Norman-Meyer appreciated that fact.
Leroy, in fact, was just about the most exotic and fascinating

human being Norman-Meyer had ever encountered in his full nine years. There was, to be sure, one Sylvia Feldnick, the cute little dark-haired girl at school with the raisin-sized boil on her nose. But as fetching and curious as Sylvia was—and Sylvia, by the way, liked Norman-Meyer, cooties and all—there was no competition: Norman-Meyer had never seen anyone with Leroy's complexion, cachet, and style up close before. And never before had he witnessed the magic a skilled craftsman could make with his hands and some tools.

So from time to time, Norman-Meyer would come over and visit with Leroy and me. He'd sit on the stairwell and watch while Leroy hammered up two-by-fours or rip-cut wood panels or pencil-measured the placement of tiles to cover the floor. Leroy was a meticulous, conscientious laborer who worked with a precision that Norman-Meyer, a boy of considerable deliberation and mental acuity, truly appreciated. So Norman-Meyer's admiration and affection for Leroy only grew with each visit.

On that day in October 1961—on the eve of the Watson move-in—Norman-Meyer, Leroy, and I were in the basement, pondering the artistic and architectural challenges of blending the floor-tile pattern with seams in the wood-panel walls.

"Mr. Leroy," Norman-Meyer asked, "are there boys like me where you come from?"

"What you mean, you?" Leroy responded.

"Boys like me, Mr. Leroy. You know. Shinier than you."

"White-skinned boys, you mean?"

"Uh-huh."

"Sure there are. Lordie Lord, you people are everywhere."

Norman-Meyer thought for a moment. "How come I'm so light and you're so dark?"

Leroy put down his hammer and looked at Norman-Meyer. "Child," he said, "let me ask you something. What do you got there inside your head?"

Norman-Meyer considered the question. "A brain," he responded.

"Me too," Leroy said. "And what about inside your chest there. You got two lungs and a heart, just like me?"

"I guess so," Norman-Meyer said.

"How many toes you got on those two feet of yours?"

"Ten."

"And he's got a big fat belly too!" I added, not wanting to miss an opportunity to help Leroy make his point.

"That he does, that he does," Leroy said, laughing. Then he raised his shirt and searched for some fat on the side of his waist, which he pinched between a thumb and a finger and displayed to Norman-Meyer. "I got some belly here, me too," he said.

He handed Norman-Meyer his hammer and held up a nail. "You take this nail here and put it right into that piece of wood there, okay?"

Norman-Meyer hopped off the stairs, grabbed the nail, and whacked it home into a vertical post in the corner of the basement.

"Ça c'est bon. Now you, Tee Robert, you do the same thing with this nail here."

He pointed to a spot on the wood post next to Norman-Meyer's nail. I took the hammer and drove my nail into place.

Then Leroy took a third nail and hammered it into position above the two that Norman-Meyer and I had already put there, forming a triangle.

"We all nail pretty good," he said. "And we all got brains and lungs and hearts and toes and we even got bellies, though Norman-Meyer is particular blessed in that regard. So I guess, besides our skin, we all basically pretty much the same, no? 'Cept, of course, nobody believes that. I ain't sure I do, me. But you all believe it, ain't that the truth?"

Norman-Meyer looked at Leroy, then at me.

"I guess so," he said, grinning. "Can I hammer another nail, Mr. Leroy? Please?" Norman-Meyer asked.

"Sure you can," Leroy said, handing Norman-Meyer the tools.

Norman-Meyer took them, paused, then turned on his heels to where I was standing. He raised his arms, hammer in one hand, nail in the other, and crouched, like a fat little bullfrog, ready to pounce.

"Faster than a speeding bullet!" he yelled, jumping up and down, all frenzylike. "More powerful than a locomotive! Able to leap tall buildings in a single bound! Able to hammer nails wherever he wants! It's Superman, and he wants YOU!"

Norman-Meyer let out a howl, laughed with delight, and took off after me with a speed and deliberation that, had he been there, Clark Kent himself would have envied. I was stunned for a moment, by the unexpectedness of it all. But clearly the hammer had had an empowering effect on Norman-Meyer—a reverse sort of kryptonite, I reckoned—and fearing for my life, I took off on the run.

"Aiyee!" I shouted, scampering around the basement, laughing uncontrollably along with Norman-Meyer, as he chased me in circles, through heaps of linoleum tiles and piles of lumber, over mounds of sawdust all over the place.

We were having great fun, and in so doing, knocked loose a couple of wall panels, dislodged a dozen floor tiles that hadn't yet set, and pretty much tossed Leroy's workplace on its head.

Leroy was furious and nearly turned white in the face. "God-damn y'all!" he shouted in a voice so sharp and loud that it carried throughout the house. "You all put me back a half day!" And he grabbed us both tightly by the collar, disarmed Norman-Meyer, and hauled us upstairs.

"Mistress," he said to my mom, "sorry to bother you, but these two here need to take their enthusiasm someplace else."

"Boys," my mom said, "go outside now and play, and don't bother Leroy anymore. He has work to do. And Leroy," she added, "don't you ever yell at the children again."

So we charged out the door and carried the game to the front lawn, then over the fence and into the backyard, where we ran and we ran, into an arboreal thicket, bushwhacking on the fly through the sappy, green curtain of long, drooping tears that the big, old willow had wept in the years it had stood there, undisturbed. And the tree, set in its ways and rankled by the intrusion, stuck out a root and caught me by the foot as I bolted about, and I fell to the ground, where Norman-Meyer jumped me, and the weight of the impact dazed us both, and muffled our laughter, at least for a moment. But we quickly recovered, and giggled some more, and lay there, our backs to the grass, catching our breath, staring up at the sky, where a sheaf of nimbus was gathering to the west.

"Bobby," Norman-Meyer said, "you know, my dad told me there's somebody else like Leroy who wants to come here to Skokie."

"To work on another basement?" I asked.

"No, I think to stay here."

"To stay where?"

"On Kildare Street."

Norman-Meyer rolled over and propped himself up on his elbows. He poked at his tortoise-shell glasses, which had slid down his nose.

"My dad told me that if the man like Leroy tries to come here, there's going to be trouble," he said.

"You wanna go over there?" I asked.

"Where?"

"To the house on Kildare Street."

"No," Norman-Meyer said, "I don't want to get into trouble."

"Listen, Norman-Meyer," I said. "You won't get into trouble. I promise. And besides, Kildare Street is close by. We'll just go for a walk to see what's happening. Okay?"

"I don't know," Norman-Meyer said. "It's getting dark. I ought to go home."

"Come on, don't be a cootie," I said encouragingly.

Norman-Meyer glanced up at the sky, considered his options, sighed, and assented.

"Okay," he said, lumbering to his feet.

Then he paused, smiled, lifted both arms to the incoming clouds, and shouted: "Superman is victorious!" And he jumped on me one more time for good measure.

Then we both dusted off, exited the backyard, turned right at the sidewalk that fronted my house, and traversed the six short blocks to Kildare Street, where we found Grandpa Abe, standing alone, as Joseph Ashkenaz and some three dozen citizens howled at a split-level home of common design, with a front door, distinctive to Skokie, that faced to the side, averting its glance out of fear from the gathering crowd.

Morton and Reva were terrified. They peered at the mob through the living room curtain, which they'd closed when the demonstration began. Reva kept thinking of Auschwitz. Morton held onto her, and didn't know quite what to think. Both of them stood there, shaking.

Grandpa Abe had caught sight of me and Norman-Meyer as soon as we'd reached the scene.

"Boys," he said tersely, "what are you doing here?"

"We were just walking, Grandpa," I said.

Abe told us to go away. I could tell that he meant it. We retreated, but only a few yards, to the opposite side of the street, where we took shelter behind a parked car.

"I want to go home," Norman-Meyer said, seizing my hand. He feared that his father had seen him, which wasn't the case, and he was quite scared.

"No," I said. "My grandpa is here, and I want to be sure he's okay. We'll be fine over here. Now get down and keep quiet."

The crowd milled in front of the home, like a cluster of gnats on a hot summer's day. Then, egged on by Joseph, they proceeded to march around the house, screaming and hurling epithets and obscenities as they circled the grounds. Around and around they went—four, five, six, seven times—the rhetoric escalating with each passing loop.

"Dirty fucking commies!" they yelled.

"Nigger lover!"

"Go back to Auschwitz!"

"We don't need Jews like you!"

Someone tossed a brick through the front picture window. The shattering glass missed Morton and Reva, who'd fled to the basement, where they thought they'd be more secure. But the sound of the window collapsing above them—the icy, shrill riff of the cascading shards—only sharpened the panic they felt at that moment.

Abe remained in front of the house, frozen in place on the sidewalk. The crash of the brick and the splintering glass were too much. He wanted to leave.

He'd come to Kildare Street because Morton and Reva were there, and he feared for their safety. It's not that he favored the game they were playing, and he genuinely questioned the wisdom of black people moving to Skokie. But the Silvers were friends, and Abe was a man of integrity. In short, he believed that by showing up, he was doing the right thing. But now that he was there, all he could do was stare, in disbelief, at the clutter before him. He was of no help to the Silvers at all.

A handful of passersby had gathered by now, and the sidewalk where Abe stood had filled with people. When the window collapsed, a Kildare Street resident named Aaron Stein intervened.

"What in the hell is wrong with you people?" Aaron shouted. "This has gone way too far! Get the fuck out of here and leave those people alone!"

Aaron, a strapping young man who worked out with weights, stalked up to Joseph Ashkenaz and grabbed him, with both hands, by the front of his shirt.

"I don't know who the fuck you are, old man, but get the hell out of this neighborhood, right now!" Aaron said.

He shoved Joseph forward, and Joseph fell backward, stumbling to the ground. Norman-Meyer watched it all from across the street, silent and transfixed. When his father fell, he squeezed my hand tighter, closed his eyes, drew a deep breath, and suddenly—and I swear this part is true—he started to chant, softly, like a synagogue worshiper at Sabbath prayer.

"More powerful than a speeding bullet," he said. "Able to leap tall buildings in a single bound." Again: "More powerful than a speeding bullet. Able to leap tall buildings in a single bound." Yet again: "More powerful than a speeding bullet. Able to leap tall buildings in a single bound." And he let go of my hand and bounded across the street with a fortitude few who were there that evening would forget.

The mob, which Aaron Stein had already flustered, was completely perplexed by the red-haired, fleshy young man with the barrel-lens glasses who'd appeared in their midst.

"I'm Superman. I'm Superman," the young man kept crowing, to the amazement of one and all. "I'm Superman. I'm Superman. Get out of the way!"

The crowd broke apart as Norman-Meyer plowed through it, heading straight dead away for his dad on the ground. When he reached his father, Joseph just sat there, glancing up at his

son with a flicker of thanks, then a gaze of resentment that
stopped Norman-Meyer cold. Norman-Meyer had seen that
look before, so he backed off.

"Papa," Norman-Meyer said, "I think we should go home."

Norman-Meyer bent down and helped Joseph up from the
ground. The mob, its engine choked, had lost its craving for
mischief, and began to disperse. Norman-Meyer and Joseph
moved to the sidewalk and walked down the street to the end of
Kildare, where they turned left on Jarvis and made their way
home, Joseph a step ahead of his son, who trudged behind, filled
with uncertainty.

Abe turned around and saw that I was still there, on the other
side of the street, behind the car. He walked over to me, took
my hand, recrossed the street, and led me up to the side en-
trance of the house on Kildare. Morton and Reva were in the
foyer, behind the door. Morton let us inside, nodded a greeting,
but otherwise said nothing. His wife was still shaking, and his
face was pallid.

I noticed the home was empty, without any furniture. Morton and Reva went into the kitchen, where they sat down on the
floor, leaning their backs against a barren wall. A bottle of
seltzer stood on the counter. Abe grabbed it, along with some
paper cups that were there, and squeezed the trigger. The noz-
zle whooshed as the cups filled with carbonated liquid. He
handed the drinks to his friends, and sat down beside them.

"The Watsons will move in tomorrow," Morton said.

"I see," Abe replied.

The two of them sipped from their cups. Reva put hers
down, looked over at me, and started to cry. Tears of catharsis
from what had transpired that day slipped down her cheeks.

Morton put his arm around his wife, then glanced at the
shattered living room window, which he could see from his
perch on the kitchen floor.

He thought for a moment. Then the smallest of smiles appeared on his face. *"Gut yontif,"* Morton said, looking at Abe. "Happy holiday."

By then the sun had set, and Simchas Torah had officially begun.

Abe stared at the window, then at the floor. *"Gut yontif,"* he said softly.

"Today was my birthday," Morton remarked. "Did you know that, Abe? That today was my birthday? It was quite a birthday, don't you think?"

"I didn't know," Abe said. "I'd forgotten. Happy birthday then, too." And he lifted his cup in salute to Morton. *"L'chaim,"* Abe said.

"Thank you," Morton said. *"L'chaim."*

"Some birthday." Reva was beginning to find her composure. "Some horrible birthday," she said. She sighed, wiped her eyes, then leaned over and placed her head on her husband's lap. Morton stroked her hair.

"Everything will be okay," he said.

And the three of them sat there, alone with their thoughts, on the eve of the day that the Watsons arrived, on the eve of the day that our village confronted the fact of its integration.

The moving van pulled up the next morning. Four black men jumped out and began to unload its contents. Willie Watson was dressed as one of the movers. He didn't want to draw attention to himself, not right away anyway, especially after he'd heard what had happened the night before. Willie would go and fetch Harriet later in the day, once he'd determined that things were okay.

A small group of people—a handful of neighbors, a dozen reporters—had gathered to watch the move-in. The neighbors were quiet, mostly. But the police were there too, just in case.

And they'd stay there for months, patrolling Kildare Street, until Willie would ask that they please go away.

Morton and Reva stayed over that night with the Watsons, hoping to ease the transition for Willie and Harriet. Nobody got any sleep.

The next morning, some visitors came calling: first Aaron Stein, who stopped by with his wife, who was carrying a honey cake. And then Ernie and Eileen O'Hara, and Milton and Evelyn Spitzer. They all lived on Kildare Street. And they all came by, they said, just to say "welcome," just to let Willie and Harriet— and Morton and Reva—know that this *was*, after all, a decent community.

One week later, Morton suffered a heart attack. He was hospitalized for a month and a half. The pressure, he said, proved too heavy. So his body rebelled.

As the weeks passed, the Watsons adjusted to Skokie, and Skokie adjusted to the Watsons. There were some incidents. A bit of graffiti. Some hateful letters. An unwanted delivery of chocolate skim milk. A neighbor who bought a little black dog, and named him Nigger, and called out his name whenever she strolled with the pooch past the Watson home.

Eventually, though, things calmed down. And Willie and Harriet blended into the neighborhood, developed new friendships, and lived, for the most part, the life that they'd hoped they would live.

In the next few years, other black families moved into Skokie. One here. One there. But except for the people who lived on their blocks, or except for the white folk who fled, nobody really cared. Skokie's blacks were largely invisible. And Skokie, for all intents and purposes, remained a white village. It adjusted to integration just fine.

Leroy Dalcourt never moved into Skokie. He did, on occasion, over the years, return to the village for carpentry work, refurbishing a basement here, a bathroom there, pleasing, as always, the people he worked for, taking pride, as always, in the work that he did.

But Leroy remained in his West Side apartment, the one that straddled a mom-and-pop grocery, the one with the mezuzah attached to the doorpost—their lucky charm, as his wife always called it, that signaled the presence of God in their midst.

The West Side turned worse as the years went by. Poverty ate at the place from within. Crime exploded. And so did the ghetto. In the summer of 1965. In the summer of 1966. And again, in the spring of 1968, on April 4, as soon as the news of Dr. King's murder spread to the streets.

The Jews of Skokie watched in horror as the West Side burned in the riots that followed the assassination of Martin Luther King Jr. Their old homes, their old stores, their old haunts were devastated, burned to the ground, looted by marauding gangs of black men, women, and children. Roosevelt Road, that grand old thoroughfare that once was the spine of West Side Jewish culture, was shattered, destroyed, ravaged, in ruin.

"They're animals," one of the Jews on my block remarked. "Just animals." It was a sentiment that many in Skokie shared. And a sentiment that some passed down to their children.

One hundred and ninety-six businesses were destroyed in the 1968 West Side riots. Three hundred people, all black, lost their homes. Six thousand nine hundred National Guardsmen, plus 5,000 regular army and 10,500 policemen, were needed to quell the violence.

Nine people died in the riots. All of them black, killed by gunshots, stabbings, or fire.

They found Leroy Dalcourt burned to death in the rubble and ashes of his two-room apartment. The wooden case of his doorpost mezuzah was torched into charcoal, the parchments inside melted, their ink turned to liquid, then dust.

"Hear O Israel, the Lord is our God, the Lord is One," the parchments once read. "And thou shalt love the Lord thy God with all thy heart, with all thy soul, and with all thy might."

Morton Silver once wrote that this message of love and of honor to God meant that Jews were obliged to cherish their brethren, regardless of race, regardless of creed, just as Jews cherished God the Almighty. "Love ye therefore the stranger, for ye were strangers in the land of Egypt," Moses said. A message of tolerance, to be sure, one that Morton took to heart. A fragile message, too, that Jews carry with them wherever they live; a message, like parchment, that can easily bend to the whims and caprice of the human condition.

CHAPTER 9

The Little Bird

Oh, birdie! Be honest and fair,
Tell me, what keeps you up in the air?
I would trade you many, many things,
For your skill and flapping wings;

When you're hungry, you get your food free,
In bad weather, you find shelter in a tree;
You always sing—never cry,
When you see danger, you take off to the sky;

You build your nest with your little mouth,
Comes winter, you fly south;
Tell me, birdie, what can I do,
To be content, happy and free like you?

—from "My Song to a Little Bird,"
by Abe Yellin, June 12, 1978

There were times, in Abe Yellin's war against the Nazis, when the whims and caprice and the grief of the battle made him wish he were back in Lubeshov, the shtetl of his childhood:

Oh Lubeshov, my house of birth!
Where Jews could grasp their place on earth.
The course was clear, our victories few;

There, God alone would stand by you.
But God was all a Jew desired.
In Lubeshov: no more required.

At least in Lubeshov, things were simple: white was white and black was black and equity the fool's domain. Abe wrote of this, after it was all over: after he'd bent from the load of it all, all the speeches and meetings and courtrooms and lawyers; after Justice had had her way; after his wits had again found their bearings; after he'd retired to the safe and familiar hold of his desk-chair cushion, to ponder and reflect—away from the whirlwind, away from the press, away from Frank Collin—on all that had happened.

"My uncle Simcha of Lubeshov was a devout and religious man," Abe recalled, "but his head was in the clouds, and he was prone to impetuous acts. So one fine day in the summer of 1913 (and what I'm about to relate, in God's name, really happened), Uncle Simcha came home from his morning shift—he was a tin-smith by trade—griping that the local police had fined him for some piddling infraction: he had done nothing more than block an aristocrat from entering his shop five minutes prior to opening time.

" 'I'll go to the judge and complain!' Uncle Simcha declared. 'A ten kopeck fine for a piddling infraction? This is unjust! This is unfair! This will not stand!'

" 'Oy, Simcha,' we all moaned in unison. 'You should know better than that. What good can come from a visit to his honor the judge? He is, after all, a nobleman, and a Pole with the blood of a Russian to boot. And you are but a Jew, and a mere tinsmith at that. Don't be a fool, Simcha. Pay your kopecks and let well enough alone.'

" 'What is he going to do? Bite my ass?' Simcha said, all full of bluster. Clearly, he'd have nothing of our protestations.

"So Simcha collected his courage and went to the house of his honor the judge to present his case. He returned one hour later, the seat of his trousers shredded to bits, and his courage and spirit similarly disposed of.

" 'You were right,' Simcha acknowledged, twisting in pain to examine the tattered remains of his posterior. 'His honor, the judge, has a vicious dog, and the dog likes the taste of Jewish meat and did his honor's bidding. I never got past the front door.'

"Which just goes to show you," Abe concluded, "that in Lubeshov, justice has a canine snout that bites the man who checks it out."

But Abe, of course, presumed that things would be different in America: that in his fight against the Nazis, he and he alone was right; that America valued right and reason; that the law was your friend and evil your enemy and the lessons of history heeded; that judges had no wild dogs to do their bidding here; that at the end of the day, no court, however constituted, would ever aid a Nazi.

But God can be harsh to a man who presumes to be right. An old Jewish proverb says: "The presumptuous man, even if he be as great in the study of the Torah as Moses our Master, will not be absolved from Hell's punishment."

So now, in this spring of 1978, as the controversy over Frank Collin's plan to march in Skokie played itself out, and as Abe's cause, much exhausted, hobbled from unsteady footing, my grandfather came to believe that God, in his wisdom, had chosen to punish him, for he, Abe Yellin—poet, scholar, fighter of Nazis—was, in the end, like every man, a presumptuous being; that he, Abe Yellin, who'd entered the fight so resolutely, deserved to be punished, for he hadn't been up to the task; that right there in Skokie the Nazis would take him, just as they'd taken Mary, his dear sister, in Lubeshov so many years ago; and that he, Abe Yellin, like Mary his sibling, would go without reason, having accomplished absolutely nothing.

"Oyez, oyez, oyez! All persons having business before the honorable, the Supreme Court of the United States, are admonished to draw near and give their attention, for the Court is now sitting. God save the United States and this honorable court!"

It was exactly 10:00 A.M., Monday, June 12, 1978, and Warren Burger, chief justice of the United States, was in a foul mood as he and his colleagues, the eight associate justices, entered the Court's imposing, templelike chamber and settled into their seats.

"I wonder if that son of a bitch is out there," Burger muttered to himself, as he surveyed the pack of lawyers, journalists, and awestruck tourists who had gathered that morning to watch the Court dispose of the latest collection of federal cases that fashion the stuff of constitutional law.

The chief, you see, had had a rotten weekend. On Friday, the *Washingtonian* magazine, a slickly produced monthly with a penchant for gossip and occasional chicanery, had published a troublesome article titled "Where the Beltway's Rich and Famous Live." The piece had indelicately revealed the Arlington, Virginia, location of Burger's home. On Saturday, and again on Sunday, an enterprising and overzealous member of the bar had shown up to picket the Burger residence on behalf of a client.

It was an ingenious, if unprecedented, bit of lawyering that left Burger, who valued privacy above all else, seething. For eight straight hours each day, the attorney, a portly looking, bespectacled, red-haired fellow with yellow suspenders and a matching bow tie, defiantly strode back and forth on the public street in front of the chief's house, brandishing a placard that read, on one side, "Fighting Words! Stay the Seventh Circuit!" and on the other, "Grant Us Emergency Relief!"

The press corps, of course, had been tipped off to the protest, and dutifully recorded it for posterity.

For Burger, the demonstration was an affront. The protester's indifference to proper decorum and litigation procedure was offensive enough. But the man had intruded into his personal life, forcing the chief to cancel the one social event of the year where he and his brethren could take off their robes and really cut loose: the annual Burger Barbecue and Croquet Extravaganza, which had been scheduled to take place that Sunday on Burger's spacious front lawn.

The chief hated to call the function off—his wife, Elvira, a croquet zealot, especially looked forward to it each June—but he figured he had no choice: the last thing he wanted to see was an embarrassing photo on the front page of the *Washington Post* of Thurgood Marshall or Harry Blackmun in plaid shorts and black socks with barbecue dribbling down their chins whacking their mallets at wooden balls while a nearby crusader exercised his First Amendment rights on behalf of a downtrodden client. So the Sunday extravaganza was cancelled, and the chief's weekend pretty much ruined.

The next morning, Monday, as court convened, Burger was still fuming. He scanned the Court's chamber one last time, but still couldn't find the offending attorney. "No matter," the chief thought. "He'll get the bad news soon enough. The bastard."

Burger opened a folder that lay on the bench before him, and looked through a list of case names and numbers. The folder contained the "orders" that the Court would issue that day: dispositions of appeals that the justices, for one reason or another, would not hear. At the top of the list was case number A-1037 (77–1736)—*Abe Yellin and the Village of Skokie, Illinois vs. Frank Collin and the National Socialist Party of America.*

The case, in its latest form, had arrived on Burger's desk just three days earlier, after a long ride through the state and federal

courts in Illinois. This was, of course, the famous "Nazi" case—
that's what everyone called it, the media, the public, even the
justices. The plaintiff, as everyone knew, was an elderly Jewish
gentleman named Abe Yellin. Abe's coappellant in the controversy was the Skokie Board of Trustees, the well-intentioned village council that had tried, along with Abe, to shield Skokie's
Jews from revisiting the trauma of the Holocaust.

Abe and the village had joined forces under the legal direction of the red-haired counsel who'd picketed Burger's home.
For the past year the parties had run from courtroom to courtroom in an emotional and costly campaign to prevent the defendant in this case, a brownshirted, jackbooted protégé of
Hitler named Frank Collin, from parading the swastika through
the middle of their town, where thousands of death camp survivors and victims' families lived. Abe Yellin and a well-directed
projectile had stopped Collin, at least initially, from assaulting
the village. But then came the ACLU, and its attorney, Steven
Klein, who successfully wrapped the Nazi in the First Amendment and chalked up one legal victory after another.

For Abe Yellin and Skokie, the last and most devastating defeat had come three weeks earlier, on May 22. The United
States Court of Appeals for the Seventh Circuit, which is based
in Illinois, held unequivocally that Frank Collin had a constitutionally protected right, under the First Amendment, to rally in
front of Skokie's Village Hall. The court said that Skokie had
acted illegally by passing a series of restrictive ordinances designed to prevent the Nazi march. "Legislating against the content of First Amendment activity launches the government on
a slippery and precarious path," the court said. "Above all else,
the First Amendment means that government has no power
to restrict expression because of its message, ideas, or subject
matter."

The Seventh Circuit also rejected the argument, vigorously

put forward by the plaintiffs' attorney, that the First Amendment's free speech guarantees did not apply in this case; that the swastika is such a lewd, obscene, and insulting symbol that its very display would injure Skokie's Jewish residents and tend to incite them to violence. The attorney had argued that the swastika is the visual equivalent of "fighting words," which the Supreme Court, in a case called *Chaplinsky vs. the State of New Hampshire,* had declared unworthy of constitutional protection.

The judges of the Seventh Circuit didn't buy it. A Nazi demonstration, they said, would, as contended, probably disturb many of Skokie's residents. But, they said, "it is firmly settled that under our Constitution the public expression of ideas may not be prohibited merely because the ideas are themselves offensive to some of their hearers."

On May 30, eight days after the Seventh Circuit released its opinion, the Village of Skokie issued Frank Collin a permit to stage a rally at Village Hall. The rally date: Sunday, June 25. One local journalist likened the move to forced self-mutilation. At the same time, village officials pointedly granted a coalition of Jewish groups permission to mount a counterdemonstration on the same day, at the same time.

On the morning of Friday, June 9, Norman-Meyer Ashkenaz flew to Washington, D.C. On the ninety-minute ride from Chicago, he discovered the latest edition of the *Washingtonian* tucked inside the pocket of the seat in front of him. After Norman-Meyer arrived at National Airport, he swallowed a couple of hot dogs, hailed a cab, and headed across the Potomac River to the Supreme Court. There, the lawyer for Abe Yellin and the Village of Skokie played the final hand in the legal battle against Frank Collin: an eleventh-hour written appeal for emergency relief to stay the Seventh Circuit's decision.

"The national attention this case has engendered and the intensity of passion which it has aroused have made it certain that a massive confrontation will occur in Skokie on June 25th if the Nazi rally goes forward," Norman-Meyer wrote. "A Nazi march would reach beyond fighting words," he said. "It would represent a deliberate provocation, an intentional incitement to riot. Such action does not warrant First Amendment protection. Therefore, this Honorable Court should hold the Seventh Circuit Court of Appeal's decision in abeyance."

On the following Monday morning, Jane Pauley interviewed Norman-Meyer on the *Today Show*. Reporters later staked out the Dunkin' Donuts by his hotel. Strangers stopped him on the street to shake his hand. Norman-Meyer Ashkenaz was no longer a cootie. He had, as they say, arrived.

The *Washington Post* had printed a two-column article that morning about his weekend protest at Chief Justice Burger's house. The article's headline read: "Skokie Brings Nazi Case to Burger's Front Door." An accompanying photo showed Norman-Meyer standing with his fist in the air outside the Burger mansion. The article quoted an anonymous White House source as saying, "This young lawyer should be an example to us all. If his brash and unorthodox actions succeed, there will be a place for him in the Justice Department. Lord knows it's time that America stood up like this man did and be counted."

Warren Burger, however, and the honorable Supreme Court, put an end to all that.

As the court session got under way, the chief justice addressed the crowd.

"We have issued orders today," Burger said, "and we are instructing the clerk of the Court to release them."

Downstairs from the courtroom, in the clerk's office, Norman-Meyer Ashkenaz and a swarm of reporters and law firm couriers pushed and pulled to get at the documents, which a beleaguered court staffer was handing out. The process was messy, and being unfamiliar with the ritual, Norman-Meyer was jostled about in a stampede of anxious, outstretched arms and elbows. He finally procured what he needed, thanks to the kindness of a sympathetic Associated Press reporter, and exited the clerk's office for a nearby hallway. There, he read the Court's order in the case of *Yellin and Skokie vs. Frank Collin*.

Norman-Meyer blinked and slumped in a heap to the ground. His tortoise-shell glasses fell to the tip of his nose and dangled there, pathetically awry. A wire-service photographer captured the moment, and the picture appeared in newspapers around the country the next day. It was a public humiliation that no one deserved.

The justices, by a vote of seven to two, had dismissed Norman-Meyer's plea with thirty-four words and no explanation: "Application for stay of mandate or, in the alternative, for stay of enforcement of judgment pending action on petition for certiorari, presented to Chief Justice Burger and by him referred to the Court, denied."

The Nazis, the Court said, finally and irrevocably, could march.

That evening, back in Skokie, the village began to prepare for war.

The mayor held a press conference, and everyone was there: outraged rabbis and angry councilmen, militant merchants and concerned housewives, reporters and TV crews from all over the globe. Even Reb Rappoport, the itinerant Orthodox beggar who was well into his nineties, showed up, wildly flailing his walking cane toward the heavens and promising *"tui, tui, tui!"* to kick the crotch of any Nazi who dared to cross his path. The rebbe had to be restrained, most gently, by local police.

Next to the mayor stood Martin Singer, head of the Korczak Unit—the Holocaust survivor group that had funded the legal and political effort to keep Frank Collin out of Skokie. Rabbi

Glickman of Temple Shalom was also there. My grandpa Abe Yellin was absent.

Rabbi Glickman began with a prayer, the Jewish benediction on hearing bad tidings: "Blessed art Thou, Lord our God, King of the universe, the true Judge."

The mayor then spoke. He denounced the Supreme Court's action, but promised to abide by its decision. He said Frank Collin and his Nazi followers would be allowed to stage their rally outside Village Hall. The counterdemonstration, he said, would take place at arm's length, a few blocks away, at the high school athletic field.

The mayor warned of the threat of violence. The counterdemonstration was expected to draw fifty thousand people, he said. Passions were white-hot, and the law enforcement challenge would be overwhelming.

The mayor said that the governor would order the National Guard to Skokie to maintain order. State, county, and local police would also be out in force. Medical emergency vehicles would be readied, and hospital emergency services prepared.

"We will be equipped to handle any contingency," the mayor said.

Although the Nazis and counterdemonstrators would mostly be kept apart, Martin Singer announced that a small delegation of community leaders *would* confront Frank Collin on the steps at Village Hall. The group, he said, would be led by Abe Yellin, "who," Martin said, "regrets that he is unable to be here with us tonight."

"Our purpose will be to remember the people who died in the Holocaust," Martin said. "We will stand there, in the Nazis' midst, and Abe will carry the Torah and lead us in the Kaddish, the prayer for the dead. And we will pray quietly, passively, facing east toward Jerusalem, toward the Wailing Wall, where the souls of our ancestors still live, and where the cries of the martyrs who perished have settled and echo, silently, still for the ages."

Steven Klein did not attend the mayor's press conference. Had he dared to show up, he'd probably have been beaten.

Klein—"the treacherous Jew," as my grandpa described him, who'd abandoned his people to defend Frank Collin—had gotten word of the Supreme Court's action by 10:30 A.M. that day. The Washington branch of the ACLU had called him at the group's Chicago office to convey the good news.

For Klein it was complete vindication. He'd had a miserable year as Frank Collin's lawyer, as difficult as any he'd ever had. He joked later that the whole experience had been like hiking down a well-sodden horse trail: wherever he stepped he was soiled in dung, and whomever he met along the way said he smelled like shit. At countless appearances, on radio and television, and in dozens of courtroom proceedings, Klein had stood up and said, unblinkingly and to much derision, that Nazis deserve the right to speak freely; that the Constitution, and the First Amendment, demand nothing less.

The price of the contest had been stiff. Klein's ulcer, which had been dormant for years, was tripped, like a land mine, by the stress of the contest. It simply burst open one day in court. As Klein twisted over in pain, Frank Collin, who was sitting beside him, seemed amused that his lawyer, a Jew, had cracked. Klein didn't notice Collin's reaction. And if he had, it probably wouldn't have mattered, for in Steven Klein's mind, freedom of speech was on trial here, not Frank Collin.

After the surgery that repaired his stomach, Steven Klein heard from some residents of Skokie: mean-spirited messages, by phone and by mail, delivered anonymously to his hospital room.

"Serves you right, you bastard."

"Too bad it wasn't your heart, you Nazi-loving traitor."

"Don't get well, fucker."

For the ACLU, the Skokie case was a financial and public re-lations disaster. The organization had always had a large Jewish membership, and a supportive one at that. But this case was dif-ferent. Thousands of Jewish contributors—and some non-Jews, as well—resigned from the group in disgust at the decision to defend Frank Collin. The Illinois division of the ACLU lost 30 percent of its income and 25 percent of its members. Nationally, the figures were somewhat lower. By the time the Supreme Court had given Frank Collin and Steven Klein their final vic-tory, Klein had been forced to lay off nearly half of his Chicago-based staff. Klein gave each departing employee a mock Purple Heart: they were casualties, he said, of the war for the First Amendment.

When Steven Klein telephoned Frank Collin and told him of their victory, the Nazi had little to say.

"Frank, the Supreme Court says you can march in Skokie," Klein said.

"I see," Collin replied.

That's all he could offer.

Klein said later that Collin seemed preoccupied.

Steven Klein placed one other call that day, to Abe Yellin. Abe had treated Klein roughly throughout the Skokie ordeal, outraged and filled with real despair that a Jew, any Jew, would defend a Nazi. In public, Klein had always sloughed off Abe's at-tacks. He wore them as badges of honor, convinced, as he was, that his faith, which he valued, was not inconsistent with the First Amendment.

But Klein understood that his actions had wounded my grandfather. Abe Yellin once wrote that the Jews, like a sponge, had soaked up all the world's afflictions and troubles. What that meant, Abe said, was that Jews must look out for their own. If the text of the First Amendment hung, as it did, over Steven Klein's bed, then these words, from the Talmud, looked down on Abe Yellin when he retired each evening: *"Kol Yisrael areyvim zeh bazeh. All Jews are responsible each for the other."*

To my grandfather's mind, Steven Klein had broken that covenant, soiled it, in the worst way possible, by embracing a Nazi. It was that breach that had caused Abe Yellin pain. And Steven Klein wanted to call my grandpa to apologize for it.

It was a short conversation. The telephone rang. Abe answered. Klein announced who was calling.

"Go to hell," my grandpa replied. And then he hung up.

Abe then grabbed the shot glass that had kept him company that day, at least since he'd learned of the Supreme Court's action. And he drew back his head, which was already dazed, and he swallowed, whole, another schnapps.

It was, I think, Abe's only vice. And nobody ever denied him his schnapps, or reproached him his habit, for he usually drank with such humility and moderation that only a zealot for temperance could find any fault.

Schnapps is what Abe called whiskey. He imbibed it just once a week. And he'd done so for years. The ritual, which I as a child had seen many times, went something like this:

On Sunday evenings, just after dinner, with the taste of a brisket or chicken still on his tongue, Abe would sit down in his favorite chair, and Emma, his wife, or Miriam, his daughter, would come to his side.

"Would you like a schnapps, Daddy?"

Abe would ponder the question, as if the answer eluded him. Then, after a moment of thought, he'd smile and say, "Why, thank you, yes. That would be quite nice." And Emma or Miriam would vanish, just for a moment, and return with a bottle and a tiny glass cup. The drink would be poured. And Abe would swallow it, quickly, as if to conceal the tinge of impropriety he felt from such a public and uncharacteristic display of self-indulgence.

Eventually, when I was old enough, I was allowed to take part in the rite, given the task of procuring the dark, brown bottle whose contents my grandpa so much enjoyed.

"Here it is, Grandpa, your snaps," I'd say.

And my grandpa would grin at the peculiar label I'd given his drink. And he'd take the bottle and fill his glass and always—for he knew I would ask—allowed me to smell the mysterious liquid he held in his hand. And I'd sniff it and back off, like a cat who'd smelled onions, scrunching my nose and rolling my eyes and wondering how in the world my grandpa could suffer the stuff. And he'd drink from the glass and devour the whiskey, and his stature would grow even more in my mind, for I thought him most brave for swallowing a concoction that God had created, clearly, for the sole purpose of testing the mettle of his flock. And I looked forward to the day when I, too, would be strong enough, like my grandfather, to drink a schnapps without flinching. For when that day came, I would know, surely, that I was a man.

Abe had gotten drunk on schnapps only once before. It was in 1946, when he found out that the Nazis had murdered his sister, Mary, and her entire family. The news had overwhelmed him.

Abe thought of Mary when he learned that day, when Martin Singer came by, that they'd lost at the Supreme Court, that the Nazis would march in Skokie. He stared at her picture, the one he kept with him inside his wallet, and he wondered what kind of man he was that his sister had died while he had prospered, and he wondered what, in the end, prosperity meant if all its advantages couldn't be marshaled—in the name of what's right, in the name of Mary—to accomplish the seemingly simple and decent objective of keeping a Nazi off the streets of Skokie.

When Martin told him the Nazis had won, Abe reacted initially with silence, as if the message couldn't register.

"Are you going to be okay, Abe?" Martin asked.

"Yes, of course," Abe said. "I'll be fine. I'd just like to be left alone."

Emma, my grandma, was out at the store when Abe got the news. By the time she returned, one hour later, a nearly empty bottle of Jack Daniels stood on the kitchen table, and her husband had started to dance.

The sight startled Emma. A bag of groceries fell to the floor.

Abe stood alone on the living room carpet, barefoot, in a white, sleeveless undershirt and a pair of gray slacks. A prayer shawl with the word *Auschwitz* stitched on its side shrouded his head and shoulders.

"*Oy didi dum dum, Oy didi dum dum, Oy didi didi didi didi didi dum,*" Abe sang. It was the melancholy drone of a *nigun*, an ancient Chasidic song.

"*Oy didi dum dum, Oy didi dum dum, Oy didi didi didi didi didi dum.*"

And as he sang, Abe hopped about the room, like a wounded little bird, from one foot to the next, short, jerky hops, one after another. And all the while his arms and elbows undulated up and down, as if he were trying to fly, and he waved the prayer shawl above him this way and that, jumping, leaping, prancing, bounding, landing on every fourth beat—"*OY didi dum dum, OY didi dum dum, OY didi didi didi DIDI didi dum*"—dancing as he'd never done before, for he never liked to dance, with a strength and a well of sadness that came from deep inside him.

For a moment, Emma was mesmerized. She wondered, strangely, how Abe had learned to move like that, so passionately, so purposefully, so filled with emotion. "He must have seen Anthony Quinn in *Zorba the Greek*," she figured. Then, of course, she came to her senses and grew worried.

"Abe," she cried, "what's going on? What's the matter with you?"

My grandpa stopped dancing and looked at her. He clung to the prayer shawl as if it were his lover. The expression on his face—a cold, distant look—sent a chill through my grandma. Then the phone rang.

It was Steven Klein.

After Abe had hung up, after he drank yet again, my grandfather sat down at the kitchen table and cradled the shot glass in his right hand. He stared at the wall, at nothing in particular. The glass crumbled in his palm, and blood covered the table.

Emma turned white and shrieked. Abe got sick to his stomach. The wounds required twenty-five stitches and an overnight hospital stay. That's why Abe Yellin wasn't there with Martin Singer at the mayor's press conference later that evening.

I was still working in Munich, for Radio Free Europe and Radio Liberty, when Norman-Meyer telephoned and told me what had happened at the Supreme Court that day. It was nighttime where I was—late afternoon in Washington—when the call came through.

Norman-Meyer sounded awful. His words were tentative, his voice fragile, his composure completely shaken. He, in fact, had spent most of the day in a heap on the floor in the hallway outside the Supreme Court clerk's office, where he'd dropped like a broken egg after reading the order that meant that the Nazis could march into Skokie. He just sat there for hours, trying to figure out what had gone wrong, what he had done, or had failed to do, that led to this terrible outcome; what he would say to his client Abe Yellin; what he would say to the village trustees; what he would say to me.

"Bobby," Norman-Meyer said, his voice a whisper, "I let everyone down." I could tell he was struggling not to cry.

"No, no, you didn't, Norman-Meyer," I replied softly. "Try to pull yourself together, okay? You did all you could. Even two justices agreed with your case. That's some accomplishment, I think. So let's look ahead now. We've got to get ready for the march."

I told him I'd leave as soon as I could for the States, and promised to bring him a genuine piece of German apple strudel, which I'd buy just for him on the way to the airport from the bakery near my apartment. That news seemed to cheer Norman-Meyer up a bit, for he'd never had apple strudel before, at least not the genuine German variety.

"Do they prepare it with raisins?" he asked.

"You bet they do," I said.

"Great," he said, his mood rising. "Raisins are my favorite."

At noon the next day, I boarded a Lufthansa flight for Chicago.

By the time I arrived back in Skokie, the village had mobilized. Shops near the Nazi protest site were boarding up windows in anticipation of violence. The National Guard had established a command post on Lincoln Avenue, a block away from Village Hall. Local hospitals were setting up tents and a triage facility at a nearby park. The Skokie Police Department had canceled all leave, and patrols had been doubled all over town.

Rabbi Meir Kahane, founder of the militant Jewish Defense League, flew into Chicago and promised to meet the Nazis in Skokie with force.

"To every Jew a .22," Kahane said.

Norman-Meyer's father, Joseph Ashkenaz, by then a codger with a touch of dementia, heard Kahane's call, and took to guarding his front door day in and day out with a five-foot-long dust mop, which he waved menacingly at anyone who walked by. We were all thankful that local authorities five years before had taken away Joseph's rifle after the old man had shot a stray poodle who'd soiled his front lawn.

Meanwhile, the Associated Press reported that police had found a pipe bomb at Frank Collin's headquarters on the morning the Supreme Court had issued its order. The bomb was defused before it could explode.

All over Skokie, the Korczak Unit went into action. At Martin Singer's direction, Holocaust survivors, thousands of them, blanketed homes and apartments with flyers promoting the counterdemonstration. They also distributed free armbands with the Star of David, twenty thousand or more. Everywhere, men, women, boys, and girls wandered the streets, going about their daily business, the armbands attached in plain view. It struck me, when I saw them, that probably not since the Second World War had so many Jews worn the Star of David in such a public manner. And now, as then, the Nazis were to blame.

In the days leading up to June 25, my grandfather stayed home, turning down scores of interview requests, seeing no one but close relatives and friends. He said that he needed to rest, that he wanted his hand to heal properly in time for the showdown with Frank Collin.

"I must be able to carry the Torah," he said. "That's all that matters."

My grandpa told everyone, including me, that the injury occurred when his fingers got caught in a car door.

Abe had visibly changed in the eight months that had passed since I'd last been with him. Close relatives always look strikingly older when you don't see them for long stretches of time.

But eventually, once your eyes grow accustomed to what is familiar, their youth somehow seems to return, as your mind conjures up a memory of earlier years, of your loved ones less tarnished by age.

Not so this time, with Abe and me. Even after we'd settled in, with tea and jam and sponge cake and honey and hours of conversation—talk about poetry and movies and women and dating and why I'd not married and how in the world I'd let Eva Singer, *Professor* Eva Singer, Mrs. Eva Singer-*Rothschild*, get away—even after all this, my grandpa still looked different: aged, not just old; white, not just gray.

When I inquired after his health, Grandpa replied as he always did, with a modest little shrug of the shoulders, a turned-down gaze, a hint of a grin.

"I'm fine, Bobby, just fine. No need to worry."

"Are you sure?" I asked. "To be honest, you look kind of tired."

"No, no. I'm fine. Just fine. A man, you know, is as old as his wife looks, and your grandma, thank God, is still a head-turner after all these years."

Emma, my grandma, who sat at Abe's side, smiled and gave me a wink. Then her eye fell to her husband's bandaged right hand, and the smile wavered, then slipped away.

"Drink your tea, Abe," she admonished, "before it gets cold."

And Abe reached over and pinched his wife's cheek with his good hand, then did as he was told.

We spent the next week, my grandpa and I, just waiting, really. There wasn't much else to be done. June 25 was just days ahead. The armies were massing behind the front lines. Politicians and the press; clergy and well-meaning citizens of various stripes: white and black, Jew and non-Jew; in buses and planes and in trains and in cars, they headed for Skokie from all over the country. My village had become the center of the universe. The ground war was soon to begin.

The Nazis never marched in Skokie, Illinois. On June 23, Frank Collin announced that he'd changed his mind; that his victory in court was victory enough; that maybe, instead, he'd march in Chicago, where, after all, large numbers of Jews *and* blacks *and* other undesirables lived.

Steven Klein surmised that Collin had lost his nerve; that the pipe bomb and imminent threat to his life had scared him; that, in the end, Frank Collin wasn't prepared to risk death at the hands of some Jewish sniper perched on a rooftop near Village Hall.

The huge counterdemonstration was called off. There was nothing to protest. Instead, on Sunday, June 25, in the Temple Shalom sanctuary, some one thousand worshipers gathered for prayer and reflection.

"It's a beautiful day in the village of Skokie!" the mayor proclaimed.

"Amen! Amen!" declared Martin Singer.

"Baruch Hashem! Blessed be God!" said Rabbi Glickman.

The congregation sang "Hatikvah," the Israeli national anthem. And "Hava Nagilah," just for fun. And Reb Mordechai Rappoport danced the hora, with his cane in one hand and Ida Zimmer in the other. And the group also sang "We Shall Overcome," the dirge of the sixties.

And the Reverend Jesse Jackson, the civil rights leader, led that song. He'd come at the urging of his friends Morton Silver, the old village *mohel,* and Willie Watson, the black man who seventeen years earlier had integrated Skokie and who'd quietly lived in the house on Kildare Street ever since.

"We must join together, blacks and Jews," Jackson said, "to oppose our common enemies: bigotry and prejudice. Let us put aside our differences, for there is much work to be done."

When the speeches were over, and the service nearly at an

end, my grandpa Abe Yellin climbed to the stage. The prayer shawl from Auschwitz clung to his shoulders, and, despite his injury, he managed to clutch the scrolls of the Torah with his right arm to his chest.

As he approached the dais, the audience quieted. Abe turned his back to the crowd, and faced east, toward Jerusalem. And he stood there, silently, for a minute, then two; then three, then four; engrossed in his thoughts; consumed by the memories of the past year's events; thankful to God the Almighty that he'd survived the ordeal. The image of Mary, his sister—her beautiful face, so young, so sad—now filled his mind's eye.

The congregants, expecting some remarks from the man who had led their fight, fidgeted, wondering how to respond to Abe's silence, wondering if everything was okay. The stillness disturbed them, for it was unexpected, and lasted so long.

A man in the audience rose and started to pray.

"*Yisgadal v'yiskadash shmay rabo,*" he called out, tentatively.

It was the Kaddish, the prayer for the dead.

Abe recognized the voice, and he smiled. And he saw that his sister, Mary, was smiling, too.

Norman-Meyer continued to chant the prayer, while his mother, Fanya, stood next to him, gripping his arm, giving strength to his words, which he hoped would lift the disgrace that he'd placed on himself for letting Abe down, for failing, if failure it was, to win the legal war against Frank Collin, the Nazi.

"*Yisgadal v'yiskadash shmay rabo,*" Norman-Meyer repeated.

Then my grandpa, his back still to the congregation, spoke out.

"*Yisgadal v'yiskadash shmay rabo!*" he shouted.

And the entire assembly repeated his words.

"*B'olmo di v'ro khirusay, v'yamlikh malkhusay!*" Norman-Meyer cried.

And the worshipers followed his lead. And the Jews of Skokie finished their prayer that day, in praise of God and of those who had perished in his name. And once they had finished, they withdrew from the temple and returned to their homes, where they went about working and playing and living their lives: lives that had changed from the Nazi affair, yet lives that remained undisturbed.

After the prayer service had ended, we all retreated to Grandpa Abe's house for a celebratory meal. My parents were there, as were Martin and Beatrice Singer and the Silvers. So were Fanya and Norman-Meyer, although Joseph Ashkenaz remained at the ramparts, next door on his front porch, wielding, still, a dust mop rifle and the gape of a moron.

Abe was in fine spirits. He could roll his neck and stretch out his spine and stand up straight again, he said, for the load that he'd hauled on his back the past year had finally been lifted.

"Oy," he said, "what a relief! I almost feel like dancing!"

Emma, my grandma, gave Abe a look that spoke only to him.

Abe laughed and walked over to Norman-Meyer, who was munching absentmindedly on some nacho chips and dip. My grandpa placed his arms around Norman-Meyer's neck, drew him near, whispered a few words, and kissed him, gently, on the lips. It was a gesture of gratitude for all that the young lawyer had done, and Norman-Meyer was genuinely touched. My friend felt absolved, and he ate particularly well that evening.

My grandma made brisket for dinner, a huge, lean, juicy slab of meat, and Abe, notwithstanding his injury, carved the beast swiftly and neatly, dispensing large portions to all at the table. There were salad and mashed potatoes and roasted carrots. We had pineapple sherbet and honey cake for dessert.

Afterward, my grandpa sat down in his favorite chair, and I

suddenly turned nine years old again, a doting grandchild at his grandfather's feet, eager to please, eager to learn.

"How are you feeling, Grandpa?" I asked, taking his injured hand into mine.

"Fine, Bobby, just fine," he said.

"Would you like to have a schnapps?" I asked.

Abe Yellin paused, and then chuckled. "Thank you," he said, "but I think I'd rather not."

So we remained there, just the two of us, our hands intertwined, our voices still. And Abe Yellin leaned back, closed his eyes, and dozed off. His breathing turned heavy and sweet. And a bead of saliva slipped from the edge of his mouth.

"Is he all right, Bobby?" Norman-Meyer asked.

I turned around and looked at my friend, who'd been watching my grandpa and me from a distance.

"I don't know," I replied. "I guess he's okay. How about you?"

Norman-Meyer looked down at my grandpa.

"Oh, I don't know," he said softly. "How do I look?"

I studied Norman-Meyer for a moment, unsure of the answer, then punched him gently with a left and a right to the stomach. Norman-Meyer held his belly and grinned.

"You're a hard guy to read, Norman-Meyer," I said.

"So who isn't?" he asked.

And we retreated to my grandmother's kitchen, where we served ourselves second helpings of pineapple sherbet and honey cake, and, for the moment, everything, and everyone, felt fine. Just fine.